THE NEW BIZARRO AUTHOR SERIES

PRESENTS

# LEPERS AND MANNEQUINS

ERIC BEENY

Eraserhead Press
Portland, OR

THE NEW BIZARRO AUTHOR SERIES
An Imprint of Eraserhead Press

ERASERHEAD PRESS
205 NE BRYANT
PORTLAND, OR 97211

WWW.ERASERHEADPRESS.COM

ISBN: 1-62105-007-6



Early excerpts from this novel appeared in *Pear Noir!* and *Spilt Milk*.



Printed in the USA.

You hold in your hands now a book from the New Bizarro Author Series. Normally, Eraserhead Press publishes twelve books a year. Of those, only one or two are by new writers. The NBAS alters this dynamic, thus giving more authors of weird fiction a chance at publication.

For every book published in this series, the following will be true: This is the author's first published book. We're testing the waters to see if this author can find a readership, and whether or not you see more Eraserhead Press titles from this author is up to you.

The success of this author is in your hands. If enough copies of this book aren't sold within a year, there will be no future books from the author published by Eraserhead Press. So, if you enjoy this author's work and want to see more in print, we encourage you to help him out by writing reviews of his book and telling your friends.

In any event, hope you enjoy…

—Kevin L. Donihe, Editor

"We often despise what is most useful to us."
—Aesop, The Hart and the Hunter

"[T]he more I give to thee,
The more I have, for both are infinite."
—William Shakespeare,
Romeo and Juliet, Act II Scene II

# LIPSTICK

"I want to get my tits done," one mannequin said.

Jaundice.

That's me.

I'm Jaundice.

I said that.

I want to get my tits done.

"What for?" Clarice said.

"I don't know. I'm sick of these tits. They don't move, and they don't have any nipples."

"None of us have nipples," Clarice said.

"I know," Jaundice said. "But shouldn't we?"

"That's just not how we're made."

"Well, what if I ever have children? How am I going to feed them?"

"You know we don't feed our young with breasts. We don't even have *young*, silly."

"Well, maybe we should. I'm just so sick of these silly tits."

"But they're just as beautiful as everyone else's."

"Exactly," Jaundice said. "They're just like everyone else's. I don't want to be like everyone else."

"Jaundice, you're being really just awful."

"Besides, I think Quall would like it. Them. My tits, I mean. Whatever."

"Again with Quall," Clarice said. "You know we shouldn't be associating, or fraternizing, or… We just shouldn't even go near them—him and his *kind*."

"Why not?" Jaundice said.

"They're not our friends. They'll never be our friends."

"Why?"

"They want what we have, and we can't give it to them."

"Quall's not like that. He tells me all the time he doesn't care how many limbs he loses. He doesn't want my parts, he just wants *me*—to be with *me*."

"Then why get your tits done?"

Jaundice—that's me, I'm Jaundice—went over to the vanity in her room and sat down.

She opened one of the drawers, pulled out a small silver box.

She lifted the top of the box, pulled out a tube of lipstick.

She took the cap off and looked in the mirror.

"Well?" Clarice said.

Jaundice didn't say anything.

She screwed the bottom of the tube of lipstick and the lipstick twirled up out of the shotgun shell its tube was like.

Clarice turned away, practiced posing with sitar music on in the background.

Jaundice, her eyes were getting wet.

She looked at herself in the mirror, blinked.

She took a deep breath, held it in, let it go.

Jaundice rubbed the lipstick in dark red circles around the ends of her breasts.

Jaundice smiled and, in the mirror, I was smiling.

# THE WELL

"Has anyone seen my arm?"

Quall limped around the colony, asking anyone for help.

Everyone he passed grunted, chewing chunks of stale, brown bread, crumbs like meteorites falling from their lips to the Earth.

No one answered, most barely lifting their heads to look up from their food.

The sky was gray.

It was raining.

It was always raining.

Quall sloshed through the mud in his cloth booties, strands of rope wound and tied around his ankles.

He hobbled up and down, pulling one foot out of the mud as the other foot sank into the mud.

"Quall," Farmer called.

Quall turned his head, carefully.

Farmer leaned on his cane, limping toward Quall.

"Did you look down the well?" Farmer said.

"I didn't even think about the well."

"Some of the children have been playing pranks, throwing things down the well."

"Little jerks," Quall said.

"They've got spunk."

"Whatever."

"Let's take a walk."

They walked slowly, hobbling and sloshing through the mud.

Some children they passed played with dummy hand grenades, tossing them to each other in a circle, saying, "Hot Potato, Hot Potato."

Quall crunched his eyebrows.

"They're just children," Farmer said.

"Yeah."

"What've you got against children?"

"I don't know. I think about having one someday, cuddling with one, teaching it to talk and hobble around, to practice throwing hand grenades."

"You do?"

"Sometimes."

"Quall, you old softy."

"Yeah, but then I think, *Why would I want to bring a child into this horrible world, to live in this filthy colony, only to have it fall apart someday*?"

Quall and Farmer continued walking.

They sloshed through the mud.

They neared the well.

They passed a row of small shacks the first lepers built, long ago.

The windows were just holes where the wood rotted through.

The roofs leaked when it rained—it rained everyday.

"We don't all fall apart," Farmer said.

"Yeah, some of us die before we get the chance."

# MERCURY

"Are you feeling alright, Jaundice?" Jaundice's mom said.

"I feel fine. Why?"

"You look a little pale, dear."

Jaundice's mom had noticed slight changes in Jaundice's personality, her mood and behavior, and she was convinced those changes were having a physical effect on her.

"I'll get the thermometer."

"That's not necessary," Jaundice said.

Jaundice's mom went to the kitchen and opened a warped wooden cupboard above a rusty spigot coming out of the wall.

"Mom, that's not necessary."

Jaundice's mom pulled a thermometer out of a small, blue wicker basket.

"Open your mouth," she said, coming back into the living room.

"Mom, please."

"Would you rather bend over?"

Jaundice didn't think that made any sense.

She looked at her mom, then down at her mom's plastic hands resting on her knees, holding the thermometer.

Jaundice opened her mouth.

"Now, lift your tongue."

Jaundice lifted her tongue and her mom put the thermometer in her mouth under her tongue, and Jaundice closed her mouth.

"So, how are things?" Jaundice's mom said.

The mercury inside the thermometer rose and, before Jaundice could mumble an answer, the mercury stopped.

Jaundice's mom took the thermometer out of her mouth and read the result, more to herself than to Jaundice.

"3 degrees above room temperature," she said.

She shook the thermometer, played with it between the plastic fingers on her two plastic hands.

"Fine," Jaundice said.

"What?"

"I've been fine."

Jaundice's mom looked at Jaundice and smiled.

"Well, you've got a little fever," she said.

Jaundice rolled her eyes toward her mom, looking up but not lifting her head, her eyes rising no higher than her mom's elbows.

"You were with that leper boy, weren't you?"

Jaundice looked away.

She was ashamed, embarrassed, though she didn't feel she should be.

"You snuck off into the woods again, to see him."

"No, mom."

"Don't lie to me. It was raining last night, and that's why you have a fever."

"It's always raining."

"Then maybe *he* got you sick. Who knows what kinds of diseases he carries around in that dirty, decrepit, dismantling body of his."

"We just kissed a little, mom. I'm an adult, for Christ's sake."

"So are *all* mannequin infants. And who's this *Christ*?"

"I don't know. I heard Quall say it."

"Well, I don't care how grown up you think you are. We're at war with them. They take us apart with hand grenades, Jaundice. They collect our parts."

"That's not Quall. He's not like that."

"That *is* Quall. That's that whole colony of his, falling apart, and they just want to blow us up so they can put themselves back together again."

Jaundice began to cry a little.

She ran to her bed and lay facedown on her pillow, her wig's brunette hair billowing around her head like a torn parachute.

Her mom followed after her.

She sat on the edge of Jaundice's bed.

She stroked one of Jaundice's arms with one of her hands.

"I really like this wig you picked out today," she said, touching the wig.

Jaundice sobbed convulsively, the wig's hair trembling like black sand on her pillow, muffling something she said.

"What was that, dear?" her mom said, pulling back her hand.

Jaundice swung her head around and looked through a thin membrane of tears coating her eyes.

"I wish I was human."

# HARVESTING

"You guys going to see the play tonight?" Farmer said.

"I am," Rosko said, taking a bite of stale, brown bread.

"Count me in," Soren said, dipping his stale, brown bread into a puddle of thick, black gravy plopped into a tarnished aluminum saucer.

"I heard it's going to be amazing," Credo said, drinking yellow water from a small, rusted tin cup.

"I wouldn't miss it," Bayer said, gently rubbing his fingers in circles around his temples.

"What about you, Quall?" Farmer said with his mouth full.

Farmer's pet mannequin sat on all fours beside him, licking crumbs of stale, brown bread from his palm.

"I don't know," Quall said, a cloud of breath billowing from his mouth.

They all sat on long, hollow rotted logs around a small fire outside Bayer's shack.

"What do you mean you don't know?" Rosko said.

"Yeah, what's all this about?" Soren said.

"You got something better to do?" Bayer said.

"No, it's just…"

"Just what?"

"What?"

"Tell us."

"It's just a play," Quall said.

Credo spit yellow water into his small, rusted tin cup, making a *ping* sound.

"*Just* a play?" Bayer said.

Soren bounced his legs up and down.

The thick, black gravy plopped into his tarnished aluminum saucer jiggled and spilled on his lap.

"You can't be serious," he said.

The bolus of stale, brown bread Farmer's mouth worked on almost clogged his throat.

Farmer coughed it up and swallowed a bit, working and

chewing the rest around in his mouth, swallowing again before speaking.

"Everyone says it's going to be great," he said, clearing his throat.

Credo sat shivering, not eating, hugging himself to keep warm.

"I'm being quiet," he said.

"It's just…" Quall said.

"What?"

"What?"

"What?"

"What?"

"It just seems like more… I don't know. Propaganda."

"Propa-wha?"

"The hell are you talking about?"

"You know," Quall said. "Propaganda. Like, so we keep wanting to blow mannequins up with hand grenades."

"We don't *need* to be taught reasons to blow them up," Rosko said.

"*They're* the reason we blow them up," Soren said.

"But why?" Quall said.

"What do you mean, *Why*?" Bayer said.

"Yeah, look at you," Soren said, "sitting on that log with only one arm."

"It's not the mannequins' fault I only have one arm," Quall said.

"Isn't it?" Soren said.

"And Soren, here," Bayer said, "with his face all contorted and bumpy with boils, and bandages wrapped around his head like a goddamn mummy."

"We all look like that," Quall said.

"And what about Farmer, here," Rosko said. "The way he hobbles around worse than all of us. His leg's just about ready to kick off."

"And Bayer," Soren said. "Your head's been falling off for months. Under all those bandages wrapped around your neck, it's hanging by only a few strands of skin. You're lucky you can still heave that thing out of bed in the morning."

"And we still haven't gone harvesting," Farmer said.

"Maybe they're peaceful," Quall said.

"Peaceful?" Bayer said.

"That's ridiculous," Soren said.

"Imagine that," Rosko said. "*Peaceful* mannequins."

"What do they know about peace?" Bayer said.

"We're going to blow all of them up," Rosko said.

"They come after us, too," Credo said, shivering.

"I thought you were being quiet?" Quall said.

"Oh, leave him alone," Bayer said.

Quall looked away from Credo, down at the fire.

He tossed some small branches onto it.

The fire cracked, like bones snapping.

"They come after us," Quall said, "because we've taken so much from them. They're just protecting themselves. Some of them want to be just like us. They want to be human."

"We're going to blow them all up," Rosko said.

"You can't do that," Quall said. "We need them."

"We don't *need* them," Bayer said.

"Fine," Quall said. "Go ahead and blow them all up."

"We will," Soren said.

"And where will your children get the parts they need when they fall to pieces?"

"We'll give them everything we've taken from the mannequins," Rosko said. "They could be, like, hand-me-downs."

"For a couple generations, maybe," Quall said. "Then what?"

"We don't need them," Bayer said. "Not alive, at least."

"They'll wear out is what," Quall said.

"I heard they have warehouses," Rosko said. "Like, surplus rooms, where they keep all the spare parts they could ever need."

They all sat quietly, thinking about all the limbs they would ever need.

"It's how God wants us to be," Credo said. "Whole."

"Then why stricken us with leprosy?" Quall said.

Everyone got quiet.

"We'll blow them all to pieces," Soren said, and Rosko and Credo and Bayer and Farmer and even Farmer's mannequin all cheered.

Quall looked into the fire and saw only fire.

# MIGRATION

"Jaundice," Jaundice's mom called from the backyard. "Are you ready?"

Jaundice leaned out the window.

"Coming, mom."

Jaundice quickly found a kerchief and wiped the lipstick from the ends of her breasts.

The tribal elders—who were all the same age as each other, who were all the same age as Jaundice's mom who was the same age as Jaundice—had called a meeting.

All the mannequins had arrived.

They were all naked—sans genitals.

The women wore wigs of all colors.

Icicles hung from wooden beams running across the ceilings of Lodge III.

The icicles were beginning to melt, their drops echoing through the main hall of the lodge where the mannequins had gathered.

The elders all sat wearing white wigs behind a long table at the front of the hall before a large fireplace.

A fire was on fire in the fireplace.

The elders sat with their backs to the fire, though not close enough to burn themselves—or melt, like plastic, human-shaped icicles.

All the mannequins had arrived.

The eldest tribal elder lifted his gavel, cracked it against the table.

"This meeting will now come to order," he said.

All the mannequins got quiet and stood still, posing in curious, provocative positions they had practiced their whole lives—plastic poses, as if they had abandoned all autonomy.

"As most of you know, the season is changing, and it will soon be time to brave our quest to Lodge IV."

All the mannequins looked at each other and said, "Already?"

"Already?"

"Already?"

"Already?"

The eldest tribal elder cracked his gavel to gather their attention.

All the mannequins got quiet and stood still.

"As all of you know, we have not been attacked in three years."

All the mannequins clapped their plastic hands.

Another elder, the same age as the eldest elder, spoke: "This does not mean the lepers have ceased harvesting operations."

Another elder: "And this certainly does not mean they've had some existential epiphany, or sudden change of heart."

Another: "If anything, our efforts have increased their need for us."

Jaundice looked at her mom standing still beside her, posing with the back of her hand pressed against her forehead, as if preparing to faint.

A drop from a melting icicle fell into her mom's auburn wig.

Her mom didn't feel it, didn't move.

Jaundice thought of Quall, who told her he needed her, and she knew it was an emotional, romantic need—much more than a mere biological requirement.

Jaundice was Quall's mate.

She needed him, too.

The eldest elder spoke: "After so many years, so many generations of their kind, they've no doubt learned our habits."

Another elder spoke: "They know our routine."

Another elder: "They know of our migrations."

Another: "They know where we've been and, by now, they probably know where we will go."

The fire cracked some sticks behind the elders, and the youngest elder lurched forward in his seat, startled.

"The hell?" he said quietly.

Drops from melting icicles fell on many of the male mannequins' bald heads.

Some looked up as drops cried into their lashless eyes.

Drops trickled into puddles along the edges of the lodge, echoing off the walls.

"What they don't know," the eldest elder said, "and what they must not yet learn, is *when*."

# FERTILITY

"Tomorrow," Jaundice said.

"Tomorrow?" Quall said.

"Before the sun."

They lay on a soft patch of wet leaves Quall gathered and spread out near a small stream that flowed somewhere in the forest.

The moon filled the sky.

Through the trees, it looked like a big cork plugging a hole in the dark bottle their world was.

"How far away is… Where are you going?"

"Lodge IV. It's where we go when it gets warmer out."

"How far away is that?"

"About six miles northeast of Lodge III."

"Is that any closer to the colony… To me?"

"It's, like, seven more miles from the colony."

"So, seven more miles from me."

"I'm sorry."

Quall turned over on the soft patch of wet leaves, facing away from Jaundice.

He rested on his shoulder socket where there wasn't his arm there anymore.

"Quall, I'm sorry. There's nothing I can do. I can't…"

Quall turned back over, toward Jaundice.

"You can't what?"

"I don't know."

Quall lay on his back, Jaundice on hers.

Jaundice looked up at the moon.

"What happened to your arm?" she said.

"Some of the children threw it down a well, I think."

Jaundice giggled, thinking of Quall and children, of Quall as a child, and she thought that was cute.

"What are the children like, in your colony?"

"They can be little jerks, but they're okay."

"I want to have children someday," Jaundice said.

"Why would you want to have children?" Quall said.

"Why not? Do you *not* want to have children?"

"No. Yeah, I guess."

"You guess?"

"It just seems so complicated. Children make things complicated."

Jaundice got up and leaned on one of her elbows.

She looked down at Quall lying on his back.

"Is that why you're with me?" she said.

"What are you talking about?"

"You don't want to have children."

"Well, I don't know."

"And you know I *can't* have children."

"Jaundice, don't say that."

"I'm infertile."

"Jaundice."

"And that's why you *need* me, isn't it?"

"No."

"Isn't it?"

"We haven't even mated yet."

Jaundice began to cry a little.

She lay back down.

Quall got up on his good elbow, his one elbow left, and looked down at Jaundice.

"That's not it at all," he said.

"Then what?" Jaundice said. "Do you want my arm? Here…"

Jaundice sat up, broke one of her arms out of its socket, pulled it off.

"…Take it," she said, turning her head away and thrusting her arm into Quall's chest.

"For Christ's sake, Jaundice. Come on."

Quall sat up.

He took Jaundice's arm from Jaundice and set it back in its socket.

"That's not even the right arm," he said.

Quall leaned into Jaundice, kissed her forehead.

He kissed her cheeks, her lips.

Jaundice closed her eyes and, softly, Quall kissed her lashless lids.

He touched one of Jaundice's breasts with his hand, cupping it with his one hand left.

Jaundice cried a little more.

"What's wrong?"

"I just hate these tits."

"They're beautiful."

"They don't move."

"They don't have to move."

"They don't have nipples."

"That doesn't matter."

"They're just like all the other breasts on all the other mannequins in my tribe."

"I don't care about all the breasts on all the other mannequins in your tribe."

Quall felt Jaundice's cheek with his hand.

Jaundice's cheek felt Quall's hand with its cheek.

"It's you I want," he said. "It's you I care for. *You*."

Jaundice smiled.

Quall leaned into her and kissed her lips again, all faintly.

"I want to have children, someday," Jaundice said.

Quall lay back down and looked up at the moon.

"We should go," he said.

"Not yet," Jaundice said, and she lay down beside Quall and she put my head on his chest and she closed my eyes.

# REWARD

"I've been thinking," Quall said.

"Oh?" Farmer said.

Quall and Farmer and Rosko and Soren and Credo all sat on long, hollow rotted logs outside Bayer's shack.

Farmer's mannequin lay on all fours at Farmer's feet.

He kept his mannequin on a leash.

He took very good care of it.

"Once everything dies," Quall said, "nothing will be fatal anymore."

"Gee, you have been thinking," Soren said.

"Nothing?" Rosko said.

"I think I know what you mean," Farmer said.

"Substances, like," Quall said.

"Substances?" Rosko said.

"Yeah," Quall said. "Like, gases. Gases won't be poisonous anymore. Smoking won't cause cancer…"

Soren had a pipe with a long stem in his mouth, his lips sucking at the pipe in small puckering kisses, little clouds of smoke puffing out the side of his mouth.

He smiled and shook his head.

"…Vaccines won't cause autism…" Quall said.

"When was the last time any of us got a vaccine?" Soren said.

Bayer lifted the leather flap covering his doorway and stepped out of his shack.

"You guys ready?" he said.

"Yeah, let's move," Farmer said.

Bayer stepped in something mushy.

It didn't feel much like mud.

He lifted his leg slowly, bent it back.

He grabbed his ankle with his hand behind him and turned his head carefully around to look at whatever his cloth bootie had stepped in.

"Ah, shit," he said.

"Shit?" Soren said.

"No. Goddamn vomit."

They, all of them, laughed at Bayer's foot.

"You and your goddamn mannequin, Farmer," Bayer said.

Farmer's mannequin lowered its bald head, turned away.

"I'm sorry, man," Farmer said, laughing.

"You just let that thing throw up wherever it wants?"

"Usually, I tell it when it's okay."

"Well, keep that thing out of my yard. Christ, look at this."

Bayer unknotted the strands of rope wound and tied around his ankle and took the cloth bootie off his foot.

"Kill that goddamn thing," he said, tossing the vomit-caked bootie onto the fire.

The fire caught it, snagged it like a nail tearing into it a black hole that grew so big it engulfed the whole cloth.

"If he was any other mannequin, I would," Farmer said.

The vomit stunk like curdled milk as it burned.

"Christ," Rosko said, waving his hand in front of his face.

Bayer lifted the leather flap covering the door to his shack and went inside.

He came back out with a clean square of cloth and a strand of rope.

He wrapped his foot in the cloth, wound and tied the strand of rope around his ankle over the loose ends of the cloth.

"One more time, and I shove a hand grenade down its goddamn throat—see what it throws up then."

They, all of them, laughed.

"Let's go," Bayer said.

Rosko and Soren and Credo got up off their rotted logs and followed Bayer.

Farmer tossed his mannequin a carrot, and his mannequin caught the carrot in its mouth and it chewed the carrot up and the carrot fell out of its mouth in wet clumps.

"Good boy," Farmer said, stroking the mannequin's bald head.

# POSSESSIONS

"Mom, have you seen my diamond bracelet?" Jaundice called.

Jaundice was in her room, packing all her things.

Her mom was in her own room, doing that, too.

All the mannequins in their tribe were gathering all their things into boxes and trunks, then loading the boxes and trunks onto wooden carts.

"Haven't seen it," Jaundice's mom called.

Jaundice thought for sure she had packed everything.

Her wigs, her necklaces, her mirrors, her radio.

But she couldn't find her diamond bracelet, the one her dad, whom she had never met, had—just before he got blown up by lepers, long ago—left with her mom to give to Jaundice.

She looked everywhere.

"Any luck?" her mom said, standing in the doorway to Jaundice's room.

"Nothing," Jaundice said. "I don't know where the heck it could be."

"Where was the last place you had it, the last time you wore it?"

"I don't remember."

Jaundice looked around the room.

"We should go now."

"But, mom…"

"It'll turn up, dear. You might've already packed it."

"Maybe. I don't remember."

"It'll turn up. Come."

Jaundice's mom put her hand on Jaundice's shoulder.

Jaundice picked up her last box of things.

She and her mom walked outside.

Little drops of sunlight fell through the rain.

Jaundice lifted her head.

She closed her eyes, the wet light drenching her face.

Jaundice's mom took the box Jaundice carried and loaded it onto a cart.

There were many carts, and the carts formed a caravan of carts—a centipede of carts.

Jaundice opened her eyes, looked far off down the muddy road.

All the mannequins, like Jaundice and her mom and Clarice, had gathered all their things into boxes and trunks and loaded them onto the wooden carts which comprised the middle of the centipede.

Some mannequins sat at the front of each cart, holding whips wound into coils like halos.

Other mannequins—soldier mannequins—held leather straps slung over their shoulders attached to those carts, waiting for the mannequins sitting at the fronts of those carts to whip them so they would know to begin pulling the leather straps.

Soldier mannequins were blind and deaf.

They could only communicate by feeling each other, and they could only interpret their environments by feeling their environments.

They tapped their fingers into each other's palms, as if typing letters to loved ones they would never know or playing piano concertos for fortune tellers who had not yet been born.

Soldier mannequins were always male, somehow.

When lepers attacked mannequins, the elder mannequins sent soldier mannequins out to retaliate.

When they retaliated, even when sent out on reconnaissance missions, soldier mannequins had to grope their way through a world they could not sense.

When they went out into the woods, they groped the trees.

They groped each other.

They groped their own lives to find their way to death.

They never got there, though—not naturally.

The soldier mannequins stood there, their plastic feet sunk into the mud, breaths choking the air with cold clouds, leather straps slung over their shoulders, ready to pull the carts.

The other mannequins in the tribe had loaded all their boxes and trunks onto the several carts in front of them.

They piled themselves onto one cart at the very end of the caravan—the centipede of carts—, and they lay like corpses, rain pelting their naked bodies, waiting for the soldier mannequins to be whipped.

The elder mannequins rode in their own cart at the head of the caravan, of the centipede—the centipede's brain—, a covered wagon protecting them from the rain.

All their boxes and trunks, ornately decorated, had been neatly stacked by whipping mannequins the night before onto the several carts behind the elders' cart.

Jaundice stared blankly, not blinking, at everything.

"Are you ready, dear?" her mom said, touching her shoulder.

Jaundice smiled, nodding her head.

They climbed onto the cart.

The mannequins sitting at the front of each cart uncoiled their halos into whips like snake tails, and they cracked those snake tails against the soldier mannequins' backs.

The soldier mannequins couldn't hear, but the mannequins whipping them still said, "Onward."

That's where the soldier mannequins went.

That's where they pulled the carts to.

Onward.

# BALANCE

Quall and Farmer and Rosko and Soren and Credo and Bayer and all the other lepers in the colony, including the children, had arrived at the park to see the play.

Rosko and Soren and Credo and Bayer hobbled along, sloshing through the mud.

They said "Hello" to all their friends.

They all shook hands, carefully.

Everyone looked forward to seeing everyone else.

Everyone knew the only way to exist, the only way to be happy, was for everyone to spend time with everyone else—and to look forward to it.

Quall and Farmer, with his cane, hobbled along behind the others.

Carefully, quietly, they nodded to all the lepers they passed.

Quall looked suspiciously at the children running around, playing.

Farmer brought his mannequin, kept it on a leash crawling on all fours.

Farmer's mannequin was always a big hit because no one ever would have believed a mannequin could be housebroken—trained to behave all civilized, like.

Everyone petted Farmer's mannequin's bald head as they passed, nodding to Farmer and Quall.

The rain let up some, but it still fell.

Everyone's feet sank into the mud as they pulled one foot free, sinking that free foot into the mud to pull the other foot free, and over and over walking and hobbling on that way.

Farmer worried about his leg.

He hobbled carefully.

"So, who wrote this play?" Quall said.

"No one knows," Farmer said.

"No one? Why put on a play to which an author can't be attributed?"

"Does a name matter all that much to you?"

"No," Quall said. "I guess not."

Farmer paused.

"Anyhow," he continued, "you know Autocrates, the head of the Theater Department."

"Sure," Quall said.

"Well, this manuscript just appeared on his desk one day. He didn't get it in the mail, no one handed it to him during a meeting or surprised him coming out of the bathroom. He just came back from lunch, and there it was."

"What did he have?"

"What?" Farmer said.

"For lunch."

"Brown bread, I think."

"Nice, I like brown bread. What's the play called, again?"

"*Harvesting the Crop*."

"Oh, yeah. I'm still convinced it's some form of propaganda."

Autocrates appeared, walking on crutches like stilts under his arms, vaulting toward them as they spoke.

He had only one leg left, and his nose had long ago fallen off.

"I'm convinced you think too much," Farmer whispered, and, as Autocrates approached Farmer, Farmer said, "Autocrates."

"Hello, Farmer, old friend," Autocrates said.

Farmer shook hands slowly, delicately, careful not to grip too hard, though Autocrates didn't seem too concerned with that sort of thing anymore.

"How've you been?" Farmer said.

"Splendid, thank you. You're looking well."

"The leg's been giving me some trouble."

"Soon enough, you'll have one good as new."

"And you, as well. When did you lose yours?"

"Early last month," Autocrates said.

Farmer's mannequin scratched the back of its neck with its foot.

"Has it been that long?"

"Afraid so."

Farmer looked at Quall just standing there.

"Autocrates, you remember Quall."

"Quall, of course."

Quall shook Autocrates' hand with his left hand because there wasn't Quall's right hand there anymore.

Quall felt Autocrates' hand.

It felt like plastic.

"You should get that arm of yours looked at," Autocrates said.

"What arm?" Quall said.

Autocrates laughed.

Quall tried to not look at his nose, where his nose wasn't there anymore, but Quall couldn't help it.

He saw a little bit of Autocrates' skull through small canyons surrounding a crater of rotted facial flesh spreading outward from the epicenter of the lost organ's impact, and the skull had nostrils.

Quall looked into Autocrates' skull's nostrils and saw only darkness, and he thought that darkness was Autocrates' brain, and that darkness scared him a little.

"It's good to humor yourself," Autocrates said. "You've got the right idea, Quall."

"Are you hosting this evening's festivities?" Farmer said.

"Yes, I'll be introducing and narrating this wonderful one-act play."

"I thought it was longer."

"Unfortunately, no."

"Who wrote it?" Quall said.

"No one knows," Autocrates said, winking at Quall. "It just appeared on my desk one day."

"And it was that good?"

"*Brilliant*, it was that *brilliant*."

Autocrates patted Quall on his shoulder where there wasn't his arm there anymore.

"Well, gentlemen," he said, "I'm off."

Farmer put his mannequin's leash in the hand he held his cane with and put his other hand out.

Autocrates extended his plastic hand.

They shook hands, and Farmer was more careful about it than Autocrates.

"Good luck," Farmer said.

"Thank you, sir," Autocrates said, and he vaulted away on his crutches.

Quall looked out into the crowd and saw Rosko and Soren and Credo and Bayer had found a spot on the hill, and they all sat together on one long, hollow rotted log.

"He's such a good man," Farmer said.

"Yeah, well, if you're not careful, you'll end up on crutches like him."

"After tonight, I'm sure that won't matter."

"Why's that?"

"I believe we'll soon go harvesting."

# SKIN-DEEP

Since forever, the elders didn't want to waste any good mannequins.

Whenever lepers attacked mannequins, whenever lepers went harvesting, the elders sent soldier mannequins out to retaliate.

Soldier mannequins were blind and deaf and, from an early age—the same age as all the other mannequins who could see and hear—, they had developed other ways to communicate.

Soldier mannequins were always male.

Not all males were soldiers.

Females didn't come with defects.

Jaundice watched as the mannequins sitting at the front of each wooden cart cracked whips across the soldier mannequins' backs.

"Onward," they called.

Jaundice lay in the very last cart of the caravan with her mom, with Clarice, with a pile of all the other mannequins all lying on top of one another.

The soldier mannequins pulled the wooden carts with leather straps slung over their shoulders along the muddy road toward Lodge IV.

The carts bounced and jostled the mannequins.

Their stiff limbs clacked against one another.

Rain fell on their naked bodies.

"They couldn't've given us a blanket?" Clarice said.

"They needed the blanket to keep all the other blankets dry," Jaundice's mom said.

"Stop complaining," a mannequin somewhere beneath them said.

"Yeah," another mannequin said. "At least you're on top. You're not being crushed under the hollow weight of a hundred other mannequins."

"Please, keep it down," a third mannequin screamed.

Jaundice listened as mannequins on the top of the pile complained and called all the mannequins at the bottom of the pile bad names.

She began to trail off.
She looked up at the rain as it fell into her eyes.
She didn't blink.
She thought about Quall.
I thought about Quall.
I'm Jaundice.
I thought about Quall.
Maybe Jaundice shouldn't have told Quall when the mannequins were going to migrate.
She knew she could trust him.
She could trust Quall.
Quall was decent.
Quall was good.
Quall loved her.
He wouldn't tell the other lepers about the mannequin migration.
Would he?
No.
He wouldn't.
Jaundice could trust Quall to keep important things hidden.
Quall could keep a secret.
Though, was that such a good thing?
The wooden carts bounced and jostled and creaked along the muddy road.
The mannequins wiggled and shook, clacking against one another.
"I think I'm going to be sick," Clarice said.
"There, there dear," Jaundice's mom said.
She patted Clarice's back.
"Jaundice," Jaundice's mom said.
Jaundice stared off, not blinking, looking at the sky with the rain falling on her face, into her eyes.
She lay there stiff.
"Jaundice," her mom said again, nudging her elbow.
She snapped out of it.
"Yes, mom?"
"Help your friend, here."
"What's wrong, Clarice?"
"I think I'm going to be…"
"Yes?" Jaundice said.
"I think I'm going to be…"
Clarice opened her eyes wide as they went.
She closed her mouth real tight.
Her plastic cheeks got puffy, ballooning out.
"No," one of the mannequins at the bottom of the pile said.

"Please don't," another mannequin said just above him.

Clarice opened her mouth.

She made a sound like she got punched in the tummy and the throat at the same time.

A thick, curdled white paste of milk and sawdust spewed from Clarice's mouth as she leaned over the pile of mannequins.

Her blonde wig slid off her head as she lurched forward.

The thick paste splattered on some of the mannequins' chests, oozing down their bodies toward mannequins at the bottom of the pile.

"Please, no," one mannequin said.

He tried squirming out of its way, the paste slowly dripping down all the other mannequins above him.

Some of it plopped down onto his neck, and he couldn't free his arms to wipe it off.

He turned his bald head and a dollop of vomit dribbled off another mannequin's thigh and into his mouth, plopping onto the inside of his cheek.

"You couldn't lean over the side of the cart, could you?" he said, trying to spit Clarice's vomit out, swallowing some.

"I'm sorry," Clarice said.

"There, there dear," Jaundice's mom said.

"You're still beautiful," Jaundice said.

Clarice nodded, putting her blonde wig on as she wiped her mouth with the back of her plastic hand.

# THE PLAY

All the lepers had gathered in the park.

They sat in rows on long, hollow rotted logs along the crescent-shaped hill surrounding and sloping toward a large wooden stage the first lepers built at the bottom of the hill, long ago.

A black curtain hung from high wooden rafters, covering the stage.

Autocrates stood in front of the curtain.

"Ladies and Gentlemen," he said, "what I present to you this evening is a work so extraordinary, some of you may lose your heads."

All the lepers laughed.

Carefully.

Even Bayer, his neck tightly wrapped in bandages, laughed.

Laughing was the only way lepers lived long enough to live as long as they did.

"I concede that what you shall witness tonight is a work of fiction, but 'tis a work of fiction so married to truth it may, upon viewing, appear utterly ludicrous."

All the lepers whispered things to each other.

"Ladies and Gentlemen," Autocrates said.

All the lepers got quiet and sat still.

"I now present…"

Autocrates put his hand out toward stage left, struggling to bow.

"*Harvesting the Crop…*"

The black curtain lifted.

On his crutches Autocrates vaulted backward, toward stage right.

On stage, two actors sat at a table.

A third actor lay on the floor in front of them, near the table.

He wasn't moving.

Autocrates began to narrate:

"Their mannequin died, and they couldn't agree on what to do with its corpse…"

All the lepers in the audience smiled with big, wide eyes.

“I suggest we burn it,” Laertes, played by one of the actors, said.

“No, we should recycle it,” Mercutio, played by the other actor, said.

The third actor lay on the floor near the table, not moving.

“Why?” Laertes said.

“The soil needs to absorb the mannequin’s nutrients,” Mercutio said, “so it can be fertile once again.”

“But, it’s plastic.”

“So?”

“So, that’s not how to recycle a corpse of its kind.”

“Then how do you suggest we dispose of it?”

“I said we burn it,” Laertes said, sipping a glass of water.

“What use would it be to us then, or anything for that matter, if we just went around burning things we don’t need anymore?”

“This is different.”

“How so?”

“We can melt it down until its plastic flesh is liquid, then we can reform it into another, more useful corpse.”

“Can we bury that one?”

Laertes closed one eye and held the glass of water up to his other eye, looking through the glass at Mercutio whose appearance wiggled in the water.

“We’ll see,” Laertes said.

“Because we should probably eat soon.”

All the lepers in the audience laughed.

The black curtain descended.

All the lepers cheered.

Farmer, carefully clapping and looking at his mannequin squatting on all fours in the mud tied to a tree, felt a kind of pride welling up in him—a masculine pride, yet somehow vaginal, giving birth to little infant prides, a pride of infants, the population of his pride exploding.

Lepers with only one hand clapped that hand on their knees.

Lepers with no arms cheered real loud and stomped their feet in the mud.

Lepers with no arms or legs just sat there yelling, enjoying everything.

Autocrates raised his hands in triumph over his head, his armpits resting on the tops of his crutches.

A leper emerged from the woods behind the stage.

He approached the stage, hobbling up the steps toward Autocrates.

“Is that Mellon?” Quall said.

"Think so," Farmer said.
The leper stood behind Autocrates.
He leaned into Autocrates' ear, whispering something.
Autocrates listened closely, squinting over all the cheering.
The leper stopped whispering, stood up straight.
"Ah," Autocrates said.
He vaulted toward center stage.
"Ladies and Gentlemen…"
All the lepers got quiet and sat still.
"…My dear friend Mellon, here, has just informed me…"
The lepers all looked anxious, perched on the edges of their logs.
"…that the mannequins have begun their migration."
All the lepers cheered.
"Soon, we shall go harvesting," Autocrates said.
Farmer's mannequin's eyes got big and wide.
Farmer's mannequin thought about its family, wondering if it had any.
"Soon, we shall all be whole again…"
Rosko and Soren and Credo and Bayer and all the other lepers and Farmer and even Farmer's mannequin were cheering and happy.
Quall got worried.
He hadn't told anyone.
How could they know?
Had they been spying on the mannequins?
Had they been spying on him and Jaundice?
*Please, don't hurt Jaundice*, he thought.
He thought, *She's going to think it was me.*
Everyone in the audience cheered.
Quall pretended to smile.

# HIDING

"Mom," Jaundice called, "have you seen my turquoise eye shadow?"

Jaundice thought maybe she might have lost things in the move.

Then she remembered she couldn't find them before.

All the mannequins had arrived safely at Lodge IV and climbed out of the last wooden cart of the centipede of carts.

The soldier mannequins dropped the leather straps and fell to the ground, exhausted.

They looked defeated, lying there squished in the mud, panting heavily in the cold air, their mouths smoking.

"No, I haven't seen it," Jaundice's mom called.

Lodge IV was a kind of compound, just as all the other lodges were kinds of compounds.

They allowed many mannequins to live in one place, in separate quarters with their families—if they had any.

All the mannequins unloaded their boxes and trunks from the centipede of carts and carried them to their rooms.

They unpacked.

None of them knew about Jaundice and Quall.

None of them, except Clarice, and Jaundice's mom who was seemingly too embarrassed to ever tell another mannequin.

And none of the mannequins, not even Clarice or Jaundice's mom, knew Jaundice had told Quall—a leper—about their migration.

Jaundice didn't know Quall hadn't told the other lepers.

Jaundice didn't know the other lepers knew.

None of the mannequins knew the lepers were coming.

Deep down, maybe, they did.

Deep down, that's what they wanted.

They wanted to be needed.

Clarice walked into Jaundice's room.

"Getting settled?" she said.

"Think so," Jaundice said. "I can't find anything."

"Did you look before the move?"

"A little bit, but nothing turned up."

"I lost some things, too."

"Like what?"

"I lost my favorite stuffed animal. The blue elephant with the big floppy ears sewn over its eyes and the big trunk that curls around to become its tail."

"That's horrible," Jaundice said.

"I must've forgotten where I put it."

Jaundice sat on her bed.

"What is it with us?" she said.

"What do you mean?"

"We're always losing things, things we really love."

"Um… I don't know."

"Why do we have cherished things? Why do we have anything at all?"

"I guess it's just…one of those things."

"Things… What things, Clarice?"

"You know, things we're born with. Like traits, or characteristics. Quirks. Not that we're even born. I don't know. Just be thankful you're not male. Then you'd probably be blind and deaf."

"Why is that? Why don't females come blind and deaf? Why is the misplacement of cherished items our only defect?"

"Well, we're also too trusting."

"Okay, there's that."

"I don't know. Maybe that's what it's like to be human."

Jaundice began to cry a little.

"Jaundice, what's wrong?"

Clarice sat on the bed and put her arm around Jaundice.

"I lost something else," Jaundice said.

"What?"

"My lipstick."

"Lipstick?"

"It was in that silver box I keep in my vanity drawer, then it wasn't there, now we've moved and it's not in with my things. I was hoping I couldn't find it because I'd already packed it."

"Is this about your tits again? I'm sorry I even brought it up."

"Brought what up?"

"Being human."

Clarice stood up and leaned against the dresser, her stiff arms folded over her chest.

She felt somewhat superior—she didn't need fake tits to feel human.

Jaundice sat on the bed, her head down.

She noticed a small chip in the plastic flesh of her thigh.

She picked at it like a scab.

"It's not my tits I'm thinking about," Jaundice said.

"Then what? You were thinking about your lipstick and I said the word *human*, then you started crying."

"I was in the woods last night."

"*Again* with Quall?"

Jaundice nodded.

Clarice turned her head and looked out the window toward a stone tower standing at the far end of Lodge IV.

She saw one window near the top of the tower with no glass in it—a paneless window, like a socket with no eye.

"I told him," Jaundice said.

"You told him what?"

"I told him," Jaundice said, telling Clarice.

# ACCESSORY

On a soft patch of wet leaves Jaundice and Quall were kissing.

Jaundice kissed Quall.

Quall kissed Jaundice.

They kissed with mutual feelings of intimacy and apprehension.

Quall stopped kissing Jaundice.

"I'm happy you live farther away," he said.

"What do you mean?" Jaundice said.

"It gives me more time to want you, when I'm coming to meet you here, in the woods. I love wanting you."

"You *want* me?"

"Yes."

"I thought you *needed* me. You told me you *needed* me."

"I do *need* you."

"Then why would you want to be farther away?"

"It makes me long for you more, is all."

"Don't you anyway, *long* for me?"

"Of course," Quall said.

"You do?"

"Yes."

"I'm confused."

Jaundice was afraid.

She wished she hadn't told Quall about the mannequin migration.

She wished she didn't feel like she could trust him.

She was afraid she couldn't.

Jaundice hoped Quall hadn't told the other lepers.

She hoped her trust was enough.

Quall hadn't told anyone.

He was happy Jaundice moved farther away because it gave her and the other mannequins more time to prepare for an attack—if they even knew one was coming.

Quall wanted to tell Jaundice they were coming.

Did the mannequins want to be attacked?

Did they *want* to be *needed*?

Who was asking these questions?

Jaundice wanted to be needed.

That's me, I'm Jaundice.

I *want* to be *needed*.

Jaundice wasn't sure she could trust herself.

She told Quall about the migration.

Quall hoped Jaundice trusted him.

He was going to tell Jaundice the other lepers knew about the migration, but he thought she would think it was Quall who told them.

She would think that.

Maybe she wouldn't.

She would forgive him.

Maybe she wouldn't.

Quall wasn't sure how Jaundice would react.

If Jaundice accused Quall of telling, she wasn't sure how he would react.

It might have been a lot easier for Quall to forgive an accusation of dishonesty than for Jaundice to forgive the dishonesty she accused him of.

This was all just so silly.

Jaundice and Quall.

They both thought these same thoughts.

But neither of them knew.

And it was all just so silly.

It would be up to one of them to say or do something to keep all this silliness from getting any sillier.

Jaundice said she was confused.

Quall touched her face with his hand, his one hand left.

He leaned in across the soft patch of wet leaves they sat on, and he kissed her all faintly on the lips.

Jaundice kissed Quall back.

"I need you, too," she said.

"You do?"

"I do."

Jaundice lay down on the soft patch of wet leaves.

The wet leaves rustled beneath her.

Jaundice smiled at Quall.

Quall smiled at Jaundice.

Quall pulled a pocket knife from his pants.

He pulled the blade out with his teeth.

Jaundice closed her eyes.

She spread her legs.

"You're sure about this?" Quall said.

"I'm sure."

Quall pushed the knife's blade into Jaundice, where Jaundice's genitals would be—if she was anatomically correct.

He began carving out a hole.

Jaundice bit her lower lip.

Quall pulled the knife out, removing, too, the plastic cylinder he cut from her crotch.

"You're sure?" Quall said again.

Jaundice opened her eyes, nodded her head.

Quall set the knife down in the leaves, the plastic cylinder he cut from Jaundice's crotch stuck on the end of its blade like a cork, the moon above gleaming through the trees.

Quall untied the rope wound around his waist with his hand, with his one hand left.

Jaundice didn't help.

She just lay there.

Quall pulled his pants down.

Jaundice looked at Quall's penis in the moonlight.

She thought it was kind of ugly, and she wasn't sure, exactly, what it was supposed to do—what it was supposed to represent.

She touched it, took it in her hand.

She pulled on it gently.

Quall watched.

His penis grew stiff, like Jaundice's arm.

"Will it fit?" she said.

"I think."

"Did you make the hole big enough? I don't want it to hurt."

"It'll be okay."

Quall climbed on top of Jaundice.

He kissed her breasts.

She hated her breasts, but right now Quall seemed to like them, and Jaundice loved Quall, so she stopped thinking about her stupid, plastic, nippleless breasts.

Quall put his mouth on one, moving his lips around it, licking it.

Quall came up and kissed Jaundice's mouth.

Jaundice kissed him back.

Quall took his penis in his hand, his one hand.

He pushed his penis into Jaundice, into the hole he carved out of where her genitals would be, if Jaundice was ever human.

Jaundice moaned a little.

Quall grunted.

"Do you feel that?" he said.

"Not really."

"Feels good."

"It does?"

Quall moved his penis in and out of Jaundice's hole.

His penis wasn't very big, but he had misjudged how big a hole in Jaundice he needed to carve.

"Yeah," Quall said. "Kind of tight, though."

He lifted Jaundice's legs, set her calves on his shoulders.

"I think I'm starting to feel something," she said.

"Are you going to cum?"

"I… I don't know."

"I want you to cum. I want my penis to do that for you."

Quall moved his penis in and out of Jaundice's hole, faster and faster.

"I think I'm cumming," he said.

"Already?"

"Oh, yeah," he said, as if remembering something he had forgotten.

Quall grunted.

Just before he came, Quall stopped feeling anything anymore.

He looked down, saw only his hips pounding against the backs of Jaundice's thighs.

"What the…" Quall said.

He stopped, looked down.

"Christ."

"What?" Jaundice said.

"My penis, it… It came off."

"Where is it?"

"Still inside you."

Jaundice looked at Quall's crotch.

His testicles hung below a leaking red patch of torn flesh where his ugly penis used to be.

Quall's penis was now stuck in Jaundice, like a bee sting.

Jaundice stood up.

Blood dripped from where her genitals would be if she was human, and on down her thighs.

"I'm sorry," Quall said.

Jaundice smiled.

"No, it's okay," she said.

"Okay?"

"Yeah, it's my first period."

Quall smiled, relieved.

"It looks good on you," he said.

"I think I like it."

# ARMS

Quall thought children had thrown his arm down the well.

He hobbled quickly to Farmer's shack.

He limped inside and saw Farmer sitting at a table near a boarded-up window packing hand grenades into a tattered burlap sack, as if force-feeding the sack's mouth dark green jellybeans.

Quall was out of breath.

"Hey, Farmer," he said.

"Well, well, well."

"What's up?"

Quall looked at Farmer as he hobbled around to the other side of table, where he saw Farmer's leg was gone.

"You lost it?" Quall said.

"Yep. Not like how you lost your arm, though."

"What do you mean?"

Farmer continued packing hand grenades.

He looked up a little, saw a big dark spot on Quall's crotch where blood had soaked through his pants.

Farmer laughed, shook his head, said, "I knew it."

"Knew what?"

Farmer now had crutches, and they leaned against the table.

He stopped packing hand grenades and picked the crutches up, helping himself to his feet.

"Where's your arm, Quall?"

"It's down the well. I mean, I think."

"Is it? My leg's off, and I know where my leg is. But where's your arm?"

"I… I…"

Farmer vaulted toward another, smaller table.

It was covered with a dark green blanket.

The blanket had a long lump in it.

Farmer pulled the blanket off the table and there lay Quall's arm, covered in wet leaves, rotting and putrid.

"My arm," he said. "Where'd you find it?"

"Mellon found it in the woods a few nights ago."

"The woods?"

Quall reached with his one arm left to touch the arm lying on the table.

Farmer vaulted up close to Quall, brushing Quall's one arm left away, and he stood in front of Quall's face, breathing heavily, looking at Quall's pants.

"What's all that blood?"

"My... My..."

Farmer lifted one of his crutches and whacked Quall in the crotch with the crutch.

Quall folded into the pain his crotch felt and fell to the floor like one big origami genital, crumpling like a dirty sock puppet's face crunched into a fist.

"Shut up," Farmer said. "I don't want to hear it."

Farmer vaulted back toward the bigger table.

He sat down and leaned his crutches against it.

Quall looked at the arm on the smaller table.

He didn't know what to say.

"Was she worth it?" Farmer said.

"What?" Quall said, straining.

"Was she worth it?" Farmer yelled.

Quall paused, his mouth and eyes open wide.

"I love her," he said.

Farmer laughed.

His mannequin crawled over to him.

He petted his mannequin's bald head.

He caressed his mannequin's chin.

He lifted his mannequin's bald head, looked into its eyes.

He pushed his mannequin's bald head away.

His mannequin crawled across the floor and lay down in a corner.

Farmer continued force-feeding the tattered burlap sack's mouth dark green jellybeans.

"Good," he said. "I'm happy to hear that."

# RECONCILE

"How could you?" Jaundice's mom said.

Jaundice had been listening to Clarice's sitar music and pacing the floor—the music wasn't helping her relax any—, wall to wall, pausing to pose a moment before turning around to pace the other way, when her mom burst into her room, startling her.

"Clarice told you?" Jaundice said.

"Of course, Clarice told me. What were you thinking?"

"We're in love, mom. We need each other."

"Humans don't know what love is. How can mannequins?"

"But you love me, don't you mom?"

"I don't even know who you are anymore."

"But, isn't this what we wanted: To be *needed*? Isn't that why we're here?"

"Yes, it is. But not the way you think. We just got here. We need time."

Jaundice sat on her bed.

"I don't understand."

Jaundice's mom noticed a rag in the corner beside the dresser, all crusty and caked with what looked like dried blood.

"What's this?" she said.

She reached down and picked up the rag.

"What *is* this?"

Jaundice opened her mouth, but didn't say anything.

"Whose blood is on this rag?"

Jaundice's mom looked at Jaundice's body and noticed a small, faded red spot on her outer thigh, then faint streaks on the insides of her thighs and on down to her knees.

"You didn't," she said.

"Yes, mom. I did."

"How could you?"

Jaundice's mom threw the rag at Jaundice, hitting her in the face.

"First, you tell this Quall character about our migration, then you mate with him like you're some sort of organic, biological anomaly?"

"I want to have children."

"It doesn't work like that for us. Not anymore."

Jaundice still hadn't pulled Quall's penis from the hole he carved out of her.

She was pregnant with Quall's penis.

She thought about that, smiled.

"Wipe that smile off your face, young lady."

"We're the same age, mom."

"Don't get smart."

"Quall needs me."

"Yes, he does."

"Then what's the problem?"

"He needs your body."

"My body's ugly and stupid, mom. He just wants me for who I am."

"No, Quall is a leper. He's one of *them*, and *they* need our bodies. They don't care about *who* we are. They only care about the parts they can take from us. That's how it's been done for generations—of their kind, of course."

"That's not true. Not Quall."

Jaundice began to cry a little.

"We'll see," Jaundice's mom said. "They most likely know now we've moved. Maybe your Quall does love you."

"He does."

Jaundice tucked the blood-crusted rag under her pillow and stood up.

She hugged her mom, big.

"I'm sorry I told him."

"Jaundice—"

"No, really. I didn't mean to. I told him because, just… I miss him so much sometimes and, and… I always feel so lost and, and I thought if he knew where I was then, then…"

"It's okay. I understand."

Jaundice's mom stroked Jaundice's brunette wig and Jaundice squeezed her mom closer into their big hug.

"You do?" Jaundice said.

"Of course. You don't think I've ever been in love before?"

Jaundice pulled away, looked at her mom with wet eyes.

"So, mannequins *can* feel love?" she said.

Her mom pulled her back into their hug, closer.

"Everything will work out. What will happen always happens."

"I'm so sorry," Jaundice said.

"Don't worry, dear. We do need this. It's not your fault."

Clarice appeared in the hall outside Jaundice's room, smiling and posing in the doorway.

She looked at Jaundice and Jaundice's mom hugging all big.

"I hate to break this up, ladies," she said.

Jaundice laughed a little through her tears.

"There, there," Jaundice's mom said, wiping Jaundice's eyes with her thumbs.

"The elders have called a meeting," Clarice said.

"We'd better get ready," Jaundice's mom said.

Jaundice looked at her mom.

She looked at Clarice.

Jaundice smiled.

Jaundice's mom kissed Jaundice on my forehead.

# STONES

Farmer's leg and Quall's arm—what once were their leg and arm—, they now burned.

Farmer made his mannequin carry the limbs out to a small fire Bayer built outside Farmer's shack.

His mannequin carried the limbs out on all fours in its teeth, releasing its jaws over the flames.

Some of his mannequin's chin got singed, turning dark brown.

His mannequin closed its eyes but didn't make a sound—it never made a sound.

Farmer stood outside his shack on crutches with only his one leg left, his mannequin resting at his foot.

Bayer stood beside Farmer.

Quall stood in the doorway of Farmer's shack.

Farmer stared at the fire his old leg burned in.

"Come out here, Quall," he said.

Quall came out and stood in the mud on the other side of the fire, looking through the flames at Farmer.

"How's your arm feeling?" Farmer said.

Quall felt really just awful.

He looked at the arm that wasn't his anymore, burning in the fire, the rotted flesh curling over itself and the wet leaves pasted on, all disintegrating like paper.

"Not exactly down the well, is it?" Farmer said.

Bayer looked at Quall, and Quall looked at Bayer.

Quall took Bayer's lack of expression to mean he was maybe going to kill Quall soon.

"We should get ready," Farmer said.

"You got your sack packed?" Bayer said.

"Yeah."

"Me, too."

"Go check on the others."

"You got it."

Farmer turned to Quall.

"What about you?" he said.

"What about me?" Quall said.
"Where's your sacks?"
"Farmer, I can't go. I—"
"You're going. We're all going."
"I'm not."
Farmer vaulted around the fire and whacked Quall in the ribs where his arm wasn't there anymore to block Farmer's crutch from whacking Quall in the ribs.
"Hey, dummy," Farmer said, "I need this. You need this. We all need this. It's time to move."
Farmer's mannequin scratched its neck with its foot.
Quall looked at Farmer's mannequin.
"You've got a perfectly good leg right there."
"And I suppose a perfectly good arm, too?"
"I don't want its arm."
"Well, I'm not taking its leg. This mannequin has been a good companion to me."
"This mannequin… *Good companion*… Listen to yourself."
"Don't push me, Quall."
"How come you can shamelessly parade your *companion* here around the colony, but I have to sneak off into the woods with someone I love?"
"There's a difference."
"What difference?"
"It's a matter of equality, of ownership. You must take possession of everything you're superior to."
"Superior?" Quall said. "Possession?"
"Don't you already feel that way, Quall? Haven't you already proclaimed yourself the more dominant figure in your *relationship*?"
"No. Christ."
"So, you're not cutting cork holes out of your companion's crotch?"
"Fuck you, Farmer."
Farmer laughed.
"Pack your sacks, Quall. Otherwise, the guys and me'll slowly rip the rest of you off and toss you into this fire—limb by limb."
Quall looked at the arm that wasn't his anymore, burning.
The flesh of both burning limbs was mostly ash now.
Quall watched the fire working away at the bones, listened to them crackling, cracking and splitting in half, as if they were small tree branches.
"Move," Farmer said.

# DOMINANCE

The eldest elder banged his gavel on the table.

All the mannequins who had gathered in the main hall got quiet and stood still, posing in curious, provocative positions.

They all stood on either side of a small stream flowing straight down the middle of Lodge IV's main hall toward the table where the elders sat in their white wigs, where the water then fell down a well in front of the elders' table.

To Jaundice, the stream and falling water sounded like human hands clapping.

"As most of you know by now," the eldest elder spoke, "the lepers may have learned of our migration."

Another elder spoke: "And they will be coming."

Another elder: "We must prepare."

Another: "It's been three years since last the lepers came. We will ready our soldiers."

"We will arm them with full bellies," the eldest elder spoke.

"It's the only way."

"Their women and children will drink of the water our soldiers contaminate."

"And the lepers will continue to need us."

All the mannequins cheered, almost afraid to be so happy.

Their naked bodies shivered.

The males who were not soldier mannequins (which were few) cheered, too, relieved they had somehow managed to escape the sensory afflictions that would have condemned them to mannequin military service.

A stone wall at the far end of the main hall began to open, the stone of the bottom of the wall scraping against stone of the floor.

Other mannequins—whipping mannequins—emerged from the opening, leading soldier mannequins into the main hall.

The soldier mannequins wore only leather collars connecting them to each other with short leashes the whipping mannequins dragged them around on.

Other whipping mannequins wheeled small wooden carts

from the stone wall's opening into the main hall and dumped their contents scattering onto the floor: Large chunks of stale, brown bread made from milk and sawdust.

The whipping mannequins cracked their whips across the soldier mannequins' backs and said, "Down," even though the soldier mannequins couldn't hear them say, "Down."

They whipped the soldier mannequins into eating the large chunks of stale, brown bread off the floor.

When the soldier mannequins finished eating, the whipping mannequins lined them up at the edge of the stream where the water fell down the well in front of the elders' table.

The soldier mannequins got down on all fours and plunged their faces into the water, drinking from the stream as much as they could have been forced to.

They put their fingers into their mouths, shoving them down their own throats and vomiting a thick, curdled white paste into the water, there in front of the elders, in front of all the other mannequins, the gagging sounds they made echoing throughout the hall.

"No," the whipping mannequins screamed. "Not here."

They whipped the soldier mannequins and the soldier mannequins stopped vomiting, removing their fingers from their mouths.

All the mannequins watched in horror, not wanting to miss anything.

"I can't believe they treat them like this," Jaundice whispered.

"Just be thankful you're not one of them," Jaundice's mom whispered back.

"I'm not thankful for anything."

"Don't be silly."

"I wish I was human."

"Don't say such things."

"This is disgusting."

"It must be done."

"How can you be so angry with me for wanting to give myself to a leper when that's exactly what we're going to do anyway?"

"It's the nature of your charity, Jaundice. I told you I was in love once. My love, too, was for a leper."

Jaundice looked at her mom.

"What happened?"

"He died."

"Dad?"

"I told you he was blown up, long ago. I was only trying to protect you. Your dad didn't even get a chance to fall all the way apart. Most of us didn't, in those days."

Jaundice's mom began to cry a little.

"So, we haven't always been…"

"Jaundice, you're not the only one of us who wishes they were still human."

Jaundice looked at her mom.

"Still?" she said.

Jaundice looked at the soldier mannequins on their knees in front of the elders, drinking from the small stream, filling their bellies with water and, with their hands, shoveling more chunks of stale, brown bread off the floor and into their mouths.

"So, you're afraid I won't die, but Quall will?"

"I love you so much, Jaundice. I don't want you to end up like me—alone."

Jaundice was in love with Quall.

That's me.

I'm Jaundice.

I was in love with Quall.

Quall needed Jaundice.

He wanted Jaundice for her whole body, who she was—not just for her parts.

Jaundice had something of Quall's—his bee-sting penis—, still stuck in the hole he had carved out of her.

She was sure she could still feel it throbbing to the pulse of Quall's heart.

No matter what happened, she would carry his love with her always.

# IMMORTAL

Quall felt all the lepers staring at him.

All of them, in the woods, sloshed through the mud, pulling one foot out of the mud as the other foot sank into the mud.

Sometimes a leper's foot, sometimes a whole leg, would snap off from the suction.

Those on crutches, like Autocrates, and now Farmer, were doing their best to not sink half their crutches into the soggy ground, losing any leverage to hoist themselves back out if they got stuck.

All the lepers kept on as best they could, carrying tattered burlap sacks full of hand grenades slung over their shoulders and empty burlap sacks folded and tucked into the ropes wound and tied around their waists to fill with all the mannequin limbs they would harvest—spare parts they would use to rebuild themselves.

Quall, too, carried his tattered burlap sack slung over the shoulder with only his one arm left.

Farmer watched Quall force-feed his sack dark green jellybeans back at the colony where he told his pet mannequin to stay and guard the colony's entrance.

Farmer hardly spoke in the woods.

He breathed real hard, sometimes stopping to look around and wonder whether or not he was going the right way.

Farmer led the lepers, and he wanted Quall right beside him—both to watch Quall and to ask him directions.

Quall felt all the lepers behind him, staring.

He felt them plotting something.

He wasn't sure what to expect.

"How much farther?" Farmer said.

"I don't know," Quall said. "I've never been there."

"Bullshit."

"We always meet in the woods."

"Mellon," Farmer called.

Mellon pushed through all the lepers, carefully, past Rosko and Soren and Credo and Bayer, too.

"Yeah, Farmer?"

"Where did you find our friend Quall's arm?"

"Just over that hill, beyond those trees."

Farmer looked where Mellon was pointing.

Quall closed his eyes, put his head down.

Farmer nodded toward the hill.

Mellon led the lepers through the woods to where he found Quall's arm buried under a soft patch of wet leaves near a small stream.

All the lepers stopped behind Farmer and Mellon.

Farmer looked at the soft patch of wet leaves.

"We going to find your dick here, too?"

Quall turned away.

He didn't say anything.

Farmer looked at the stream.

"I think we should follow it."

"Yeah," Mellon said.

"Let's move."

Quall and the other lepers followed Farmer along the stream.

Rain soaked their clothes, weighing them down, their hopes heavy.

But the prospect of rebuilding themselves was greater than the gravity of their impending oblivion, enough to lift their legs and hoist them forward, pump blood through their leprous limbs, air into and out of their lungs, as if their entire bodies were involuntary muscles they would give anything to replace with parts they wouldn't ever have to move again.

Lepers wished they could be like mannequins.

Mannequins never died, lepers thought.

Lepers could only rebuild themselves so long.

They could only replace as many parts as it took to not be human anymore, until they were nothing but walking prosthetics—just all so mechanical, they thought—, but they would probably have died long before they lost that much.

Mannequins could be blown up over and moreover.

There was that rumor going around the colony:

The mannequins had warehouses, a surplus room in every lodge, somewhere in back, and, no matter what happened, they could always replace the parts of themselves they had lost.

Lepers just died.

"You know why we do this," Farmer said.

"I know, I just don't get it," Quall said.

"This isn't about love. It's not about compassion, or doing what's right. This is about *survival*."

"Survival."

"We must *survive*."

"Always the optimistic pessimist."

"Remember when you told me you thought about having children?"

"Yeah," Quall said.

"That's survival. Outliving our own deaths by handing them down like heirlooms to our children—like limbs. Prosthetics. It's in our nature."

"Because we're human."

"Yes. *Human*."

"I don't want *human* children."

Farmer stopped vaulting through the mud.

He nodded his head at Quall's crotch.

"Too late for that anyway," he said.

Farmer continued again on his crutches.

"I'd much rather have plastic children," Quall said, "children like mannequins have that aren't born and don't die, who won't ever biodegrade."

"I'm beginning to think your love for this mannequin isn't love at all, but envy."

"It *is* love, for Christ's sake."

"Funny you should bring that up."

"What?" Quall said.

"Christ. Mannequins don't go to heaven, you know. God doesn't let them in. They're amoral savages, put here for *us*, so we can cure ourselves."

"From the diseases we were born with, you mean—diseases *God* gave us. This isn't a cure, Farmer."

"God wants us to have their parts, Quall. We're made in God's image, and that image is an image of wholeness—of anatomic fulfillment and corporeal unity."

"If we're made in God's image, then is *God* falling apart up there in heaven? We're suffering. Is *God* suffering? Are we being punished for *God's* suffering? Why would God make us like this, then punish *us* for it?"

"God is perfect, and we should attempt to reflect that perfection."

"Then, in whose image are the mannequins made?"

Farmer didn't say anything for a moment.

"You know," Farmer said, "mannequins long to be human. They only wish they could die. They envy *us*."

"And we envy them, Farmer. You heard me say as much the other day. This is silly."

It was getting dark out.

All the lepers followed Farmer who followed the stream to

where he hoped the mannequins had migrated.

None of them were sure how many miles they had come, or how many miles they had left to go.

The lepers were cold.

They were hungry.

They wished they were back home, comfy under a blanket beside a fire.

They all thought about rebuilding themselves, how complete they would feel.

None of them thought for a moment they were making a mistake.

They certainly never thought Bayer would have a heart attack.

# APPLAUSE

They snuck out and into the woods early.

The sun hadn't come up yet.

Not that any of them could tell.

It was always dark to them.

They groped the trees through the woods, moving trunk to trunk, keeping their hands out in front of them when there wasn't a tree to grope.

The soldier mannequins were so full of water and chunks of stale, brown bread it hurt to move.

By the time the sun came up, the lepers were hobbling on toward the mannequin compound while the soldier mannequins, unknowingly, snuck past them on the other side of the woods.

The sun was up, but it wore the clouds for a scarf.

It was a thick, gray scarf, soggy and dripping.

The soldier mannequins all were naked.

Raindrops pelted their plastic bodies, snapping when the drops burst against them.

They sloshed through the mud in their bare, plastic feet.

They moaned, cried out.

None of them had any idea the others felt the same way: Cold, tired, hurt.

Sometimes they stopped, tapped their fingers into each other's palms to communicate an idea, to keep the infantry informed as to which direction it was heading.

Then they groped the trees some more.

They felt wind brush their faces.

The sun was already setting.

As they got closer, they thought they could smell the smells of the leper colony wafting toward them.

They could smell fires burning.

They could smell women.

They could smell sleeping children's breaths.

They stopped and tapped their fingers.

Their piano palms knew the song.

They groped the trees.

They smelled something else.

The soldier mannequins stopped—

A mannequin.

Farmer's mannequin saw them approaching, saw them feeling their way through the woods.

It began pacing at the colony's entrance.

It was excited to see something so familiar.

It put its nose up in the air.

It could smell them, too.

The soldier mannequins were confused, their bellies full, aching.

Farmer's mannequin clapped its plastic hands.

It thought about getting off its knees.

It thought about standing up.

# ATTACK

"There it is," Farmer said, smiling.

Quall closed his eyes, put his head down.

The sun had set by the time they reached the mannequin compound, its main hall lit up like a pumpkin's hollow face carved out of the darkness.

All the lepers crouched behind some trees on a small hill.

They looked at the main hall, its walls built with logs, and the roof with its big stone chimney, and there was smoke coming out of it.

It looked like something lepers would build.

A stone tower stood beside the main hall.

There were smaller cabins scattered around the tower.

The tower had a paneless window at the top, a fire flickering within.

"Well," Farmer said.

He untied the rope wound around his tattered burlap sack's lips, reached in and pulled a hand grenade from its mouth.

"Farmer, please," Quall said.

"Enough. Everyone ready?"

All the lepers untied their tattered burlap sacks' lips and they all reached into their sacks' mouths and pulled out hand grenades.

With their teeth, the lepers pulled out the hand grenades' pins and made fists around the hand grenades to hold the detonation levers on.

"You too, Quall," Farmer said.

Quall put his head down.

He looked at the mannequin compound.

He thought about Jaundice, where she was just then.

He turned and looked at all the other lepers behind him.

Farmer smiled, raising an eyebrow.

Quall untied his tattered burlap sack's lips and reached into its mouth, but he didn't grab anything.

"Alright," Farmer said quietly. "This is for Bayer. He would've gotten himself a new head tonight for when his own head fell off, but what he really needed was a new heart. And those goddamn mannequins don't have hearts."

Rosko and Soren and Credo and all the other lepers—save Quall—caressed their hand grenades.

They all felt bad about leaving Bayer's body out in the woods but, with the tattered burlap sacks slung over their shoulders heavy with hand grenades, they couldn't possibly carry him.

"Now, let our grenades guide us to glory," Farmer called.

Rosko got really into it, fondling his hand grenade.

He got so into it, the detonation lever slipped from his fingers and the hand grenade blew his arm off—disarming him.

"Christ," he said.

All the lepers leapt up, trying to not explode.

Farmer looked at Rosko lying there, rolling around in the mud, wailing.

Farmer looked at Lodge IV, the mannequin compound, and saw silhouettes standing in the stone tower's paneless window, flickering like wings of candlelight flapping on a wall.

"Shit," he said.

He saw more silhouettes scattering around the inside of the lodge's main hall and all the surrounding cabins.

"Rosko," Farmer called. "Can you move?"

"Yeah, I'll be okay," Rosko said.

"Right. Let's go…go…go…"

All the lepers hobbled down the hill.

Farmer grabbed Quall by the shirt, pulled him close.

"You," he said, "stay with me."

# MISUNDERSTANDING

"Ahhhhhhh," Farmer's mannequin said.

When it ran out of breath, it laughed.

Then it went, "Ahhhhhhh," again.

It clapped its plastic hands, stood on its feet.

Its leash was tied around one of the wooden posts of the fence surrounding the colony.

The soldier mannequins approached slowly, groping the trees.

They followed Farmer's mannequin's scent.

The women who had remained at the colony got up out of bed and looked out their front windows to see what was happening.

There were torches lit all around the colony at the tops of tall wooden poles.

The women looked out into the darkness and, through the torchlight, saw bald, naked figures fumbling around outside the fence.

The figures moved through the trees.

Torchlight flickered against the silhouettes of their naked bodies.

Farmer's mannequin stood at the colony's entrance clapping and going, "Ahhhhhhh," inviting the figures in, just so happy to see them.

The women ran into their children's bedrooms and got them up out of bed and they all left their shacks and fled to another shack at the far end of the colony.

Some women carried their children and some food.

Some women carried their children and food and other things, like blankets or wooden toys.

Some women dropped the things they carried as they ran slipping through the mud, and they had to go back to pick those things up.

"Ahhhhhhh," Farmer's mannequin went.

The soldier mannequins moved closer.

Some women running lost a leg and told their children to keep running, and they looked for their leg and some found their leg and some didn't find their leg and some found someone else's leg and hopped away on their one leg left.

When all the women and children reached the shack, the first woman inside locked the door after the last.

A long, thick rope dangled from the ceiling.

One woman pulled the rope, opening a trap door, and a retractable ladder slid down, thudding against the warped wooden floorboards.

The women and children all climbed the ladder up into the trap door which led to the attic, lifting the door and closing it tightly after them.

There, in the dark, the women groped their children's bodies to see if they had lost any limbs, hoping to find everything still there.

Some women who had picked up a leg while fleeing said, "This isn't my leg."

Other women who had lost a leg said, "Oh, I think that's mine."

The soldier mannequins reached the colony's entrance where they smelled a mannequin.

They stopped.

Farmer's mannequin clapped its plastic hands.

It went, "Ahhhhhhh."

The soldier mannequins didn't respond, just stood there, sniffing.

Farmer's mannequin stopped making noises.

One of the soldier mannequins reached his hand out, waving his arm in front of him.

He moved forward.

Farmer's mannequin looked at him, reached out its own hand.

As their hands touched the soldier mannequin stopped, tilted his bald head a little.

He felt Farmer's mannequin's plastic hand.

Farmer's mannequin smiled.

The soldier mannequin tapped his fingers into Farmer's mannequin's palm.

Farmer's mannequin looked at all the other soldier mannequins, at their bald heads and their naked bodies flickering in the torchlight.

They sniffed the air, turning their bald heads side to side.

Farmer's mannequin didn't understand what the soldier mannequin was doing.

The soldier mannequin finished tapping his fingers into Farmer's mannequin's palm and put his hand out for a reply.

Farmer's mannequin tapped its fingers into the soldier mannequin's palm.

The soldier mannequin opened his mouth.

He crunched his hairless eyebrows together.

Farmer's mannequin smiled.

It didn't understand what it was doing.

It thought they were playing a game.

The soldier mannequin was possibly offended by something Farmer's mannequin accidentally tapped into his palm, or maybe Farmer's mannequin was simply a mannequin who didn't know at all how to speak blind and deaf soldier mannequin and, so, was considered an imposter.

The soldier mannequin felt around Farmer's mannequin's bald head and found the collar connected to the leash around its neck.

The soldier mannequin followed the leash to the fence post and untied it.

He tugged on it and led Farmer's mannequin away from the entrance and into the colony.

The soldier mannequin smelled smoke.

He followed a source of heat his plastic body felt.

Farmer's mannequin smiled as it was pulled forward.

The soldier mannequin stopped where the source of heat felt hottest against his plastic body.

Farmer's mannequin looked at the fire.

"Ahhhhhhh," it went.

It clapped its plastic hands.

The soldier mannequin stood next to Farmer's mannequin and put his arm around its shoulders.

The other soldier mannequins followed them, feeling the footsteps of the first soldier mannequin jiggling shockwaves through the mud.

They all stood around the first soldier mannequin with his arm around Farmer's mannequin.

The soldier mannequin, with his blank eyes, turned his bald head slowly, appeared to be looking at Farmer's mannequin.

The soldier mannequin smiled.

Farmer's mannequin smiled.

The soldier mannequin pushed Farmer's mannequin into the fire.

Farmer's mannequin seemed unhappy.

It wiggled around a little.

The fire colored Farmer's mannequin's body with dark brown spots like a leopard bruising itself with black holes.

Farmer's mannequin stared at the soldier mannequin, feigning interest in its own pain.

All the other soldier mannequins stood around not watching Farmer's mannequin pretend to enjoy burning to death.

I mean, all the soldier mannequins stood around pretending to watch Farmer's mannequin not enjoy burning to death.

That's what Jaundice meant.

That's me.

I'm Jaundice.

What I meant to say was, all the blind and deaf soldier mannequins stood around pretending to watch Farmer's mannequin wishing it could enjoy not burning to death.

# DISARMED

They stormed the mannequin compound, lugging heavy, tattered burlap sacks full of hand grenades—homemade hand grenades they had manufactured back at the colony and stored like they would raindrops in their supply of drinking water.

Though there was no drought.

It was always raining.

All the lepers pulled hand grenades from the mouths of their tattered burlap sacks.

They pulled the hand grenades' pins out with their teeth.

They hurled the hand grenades through windows and doorways.

Rosko, sans one arm, and Soren and Credo, and all the other lepers, hobbled around blowing things up.

Quall stayed with Farmer, just as Farmer told him to.

He stayed with Farmer, even though he could have easily outrun Farmer with Farmer's one leg left.

Quall worried what the other lepers would do if they caught him trying to escape into the woods.

The mannequins fled in all directions.

The elders of the tribe remained seated at their table in the main hall.

Rosko stopped, put down his tattered burlap sack.

He reached into its mouth with his one arm left and pulled out hand grenades, and he pulled their pins out with his teeth and he threw them everywherever.

Soren tackled a mannequin.

He sat on top of the mannequin, straddled the mannequin.

He got a hand grenade out, pulled the pin.

He opened the mannequin's mouth and shoved the hand grenade into its mouth, and he got up and kicked the mannequin in the throat.

Soren hobbled away, and the mannequin's head blew up.

Its limbs flew off in all directions, and all the lepers followed and gathered and stuffed them into their empty burlap sacks.

Autocrates tripped mannequins with his crutches while Mellon tore them apart, limb by limb, with his bare hands.

Some lepers pulled hand grenades from their tattered burlap sacks' mouths and they bit the pins out with their teeth and threw the hand grenades, and their arms came off while throwing them.

Their arms flew through the air, their hands still clutching the hand grenades, throwing off the hand grenades' center of gravity—the hand grenades twirling the arms like boomerangs that wouldn't ever come back.

The one arm Rosko had left tore out from its shoulder socket, disarming him completely as he hurled a hand grenade into one of the main hall's windows.

The elders sitting at their table near the front of the hall heard glass shatter and saw an arm fly into the hall, something clutched in its fist.

"The hell?" the youngest elder said.

The hand grenade exploded.

"Oh," the youngest elder said.

The eldest elder sat quietly.

Another elder spoke: "Should we just sit here?"

Another elder: "What's the point of going out there?"

Another: "Why just wait to be found?"

"This is what we do," the eldest elder said. "It's in our nature. We will not fear them. Soon, they will all be made of us—at least, those of them who survive."

"That's what I'm afraid of," the youngest elder said, adjusting his white wig.

He got up from the table and walked around it, leaping across the small stream flowing straight down the middle of the main hall toward the well in front of the table.

He ran toward the far end of the hall, toward the stone wall from which the whipping mannequins dragging soldier mannequins on leashes had emerged.

Several hand grenades flew into the windows, landing in or near the stream.

The youngest elder reached the stone wall and pushed it open, the stone of the bottom of the wall scraping against the stone of the floor, and he entered the opening and pushed the stone wall closed.

The hand grenades floated along on the stream's current toward the elders' table where the stream's water fell down the well.

The elders all clutched the armrests of their chairs, opened their eyes wide as they went.

The eldest elder smiled and sighed big.

Just as the hand grenades reached the top of the waterfall in front of the elders' table, they exploded.

The table and the mannequins' tribal elders—who were all the same age as each other, who were all the same age as all the other mannequins—got blown to pieces, white wigs flying and water splashing all over, quickly dousing the explosions' fires.

Carefully, Credo kicked open the doors to the main hall and peeked inside.

He held a hand grenade over his head, its pin between his teeth.

He hobbled in, tossed the hand grenade toward the front of the hall where the elders' table used to be, and the hand grenade blew up.

Credo smiled at all the elders' limbs lying around, and he unfolded his empty burlap sack and began collecting what he could fit into its mouth.

Something fell, clacking behind him.

Credo stopped collecting the elders' limbs and listened.

He reached into his sack and pulled a pin.

He turned around, and the youngest elder stood there in his white wig holding a mannequin leg by the ankle, and he swung the mannequin leg at Credo, his white wig slipping off his head as the mannequin leg's thigh cracked Credo's skull wide open.

Credo fell to the floor, his sack's mouth vomiting hand grenades like dark green jellybeans.

They rolled out and stopped all around the youngest elder's feet, his white wig lying there.

"The hell?" the youngest elder said.

The pinless hand grenade rolled out of Credo's hand.

"Oh," the youngest elder said.

The lever popped and the hand grenade went off, taking all the hand grenades with it and the youngest elder and Credo—all gone.

Some lepers hobbling around outside throwing hand grenades everywherever didn't think to remember other lepers were doing that, too, and they accidentally stepped on stray hand grenades lying half-sunk in the mud.

Other lepers didn't need their arms or legs blown off by their own or other lepers' hand grenades.

Their arms and legs just fell off, or flew off, or got stuck in the mud and snapped off, and they just toppled over and felt bad about themselves.

They couldn't keep themselves in one piece long enough to put themselves back together.

# VOICES

Clarice stood naked in the window, posing with one hand resting on her hip and the other across her breasts.

Jaundice and Jaundice's mom were with Clarice, there in her room, trying to convince her to leave with them, to hide somewhere.

Clarice had a serene look on her face.

The look was unreal, manufactured, like.

She wore a dirty blonde wig, a pearl necklace.

"It might be fun," Jaundice's mom said.

"Come on, Clarice," Jaundice said.

Hand grenades went off outside, and lepers and mannequins were hobbling and falling all over, yelling things out of desperation and fear.

"No, that's okay," Clarice said.

"You're just going to stay here?" Jaundice said.

"It doesn't matter."

Clarice looked at her reflection in the glass superimposed over the landscape outside, blooming with the rose bushes of hand grenade explosions.

"I really feel just beautiful," she said.

Jaundice looked at her mom and Jaundice's mom looked at Jaundice.

"You are," Jaundice's mom said. "Very romantic, like."

Jaundice got quiet and sat still.

"What's wrong, dear?" her mom said.

"I'm wondering about Quall."

"You and those tits of yours," Clarice said. "I love my tits."

Jaundice looked at Clarice standing in the window.

Candlelight flickered like the shadows of wings flapping against her naked body.

Jaundice crunched her eyebrows together.

"What's this?" Jaundice's mom said.

"Jaundice wants to get her tits done," Clarice said.

"You what?"

"Mom—"

"Yeah, she wants to lactate and feed children with her tits."

"Shut up, Clarice."

Jaundice's mom stood up.

"I know you want to be human," she said. "But, but…*tits*?"

"Mom—"

"She wants tits and whatever else."

"Clarice—"

"You want to replace yourself with human parts," Jaundice's mom said, "like they do with ours?"

"I was just thinking out loud."

"But…*tits*?"

"Tits," Clarice said.

"Shut up," Jaundice said.

"You want *tits*?"

"Mom."

"Tits."

"Clarice," Jaundice's mom said.

Jaundice stood up.

"Mom, you're confusing me."

She left Clarice's room.

"Jaundice, come back here," her mom said.

Jaundice walked down a small flight of stairs and out the back door of Clarice's cabin.

Beneath the explosions, beneath all the lepers and mannequins screaming, Jaundice heard a familiar voice.

The voice came from around the other side of Clarice's cabin.

"Quall," Jaundice said.

# PULSE

All the women and children kept quiet.

They sat down or they stood up, and they did that quietly.

Nothing they said or did would matter anyway.

They all looked at each other in the dark, their hearts pounding—the thick, dull sound of their bodies' blood cautiously coursing through their leprous limbs, the blood confused, flooding their ears, trickling out—, wondering what would happen.

The soldier mannequins all groped their way from the fire Farmer's mannequin burned in, feeling their way farther into the colony.

Some of them bumped up against tall poles with lit torches perched on top.

The soldier mannequins got confused and thought the poles were really tall stems, their flames like bouquets of flowers drinking the rain.

Their arms fingered their way to the tops of the poles toward a heat source on which they burned their fingertips.

The soldier mannequins put their fingers into their mouths and sucked.

They pulled the torches down.

They groped the air, holding the torches out in front of them as if it helped them to see better.

They sloshed their way through the mud, the mud squishing between their plastic toes.

They stopped at every shack in the colony and went inside, and they groped the walls and they tripped over things and they didn't find anyone.

Some soldier mannequins came outside and bumped into other soldier mannequins.

They tapped their fingers into one another's palms—confirming first identity, then direction.

Three soldier mannequins slipped in the mud and fell, and they felt each other fall through vibrations in the mud—the mud jiggling hesitantly, like breast implants.

They slid down a small hill, landing in a water source.

They reached over and felt one another lying there.

The three of them moaned.

They stood up, their movements epileptic, palsy.

One tapped something into another's palm, and that one tapped something into the other's palm.

They crouched.

They all shoved their fingers into their mouths, plunging them down their throats, pressing the backs of their tongues like keys on the same piano, and they began vomiting a thick, curdled white paste of milk and sawdust.

Another soldier mannequin slipped in mud and slid down the same small hill, knocking over two of the soldier mannequins who were vomiting into the water.

Another soldier mannequin slipped.

Another.

Another.

Another.

One of them put his hand out and felt something thick splattering into his palm.

He smelled his palm.

He licked it.

One soldier mannequin turned over when he fell and slid head-first like being born into the water source from the hill's womb.

Another soldier mannequin fell, got up, crouched and, too, plunged his finger down his throat and began vomiting a thick, curdled white paste into the water, and the vomit splashed onto the one who fell and slid head-first like being born into the water source's chest.

Soon, all the soldier mannequins who slid down the small hill and into the water source made themselves vomit into the water.

The other soldier mannequins who hadn't yet stumbled onto the water source continued groping their way through the colony.

They searched all the shacks and found nothing.

They reached the edge of the colony and, still, they found no one.

The soldier mannequins soon came to the very last shack.

One of them had his arms stretched out in front of him.

Waving them through the air he found a railing, and stubbed his toe on the bottom step of a small staircase.

The others behind him did the same thing.

Some held torches they had pulled down.

They climbed the steps onto the porch and went inside.

The women heard the mannequins' footsteps downstairs, their plastic feet clacking against the shack's warped wooden floorboards.

The women pulled their children close.

One woman slowly and quietly got down on all fours, put her forehead against the cold attic floor.

She closed one eye and peeked with her other eye through cracks in the warped wooden floorboards, the ceiling of the story beneath them, and she saw flashes of bald mannequins groping the air and walls.

They held torches, the torchlight flickering against their naked bodies.

The woman got up slowly, quietly, the wood creaking beneath her.

As she stood, her foot brushed some dust through the cracks between the floorboards, and the dust drifted down, landing on one of the soldier mannequins' faces.

The soldier mannequin shook his bald head and tried blowing the dust out of his face like the hair of a wig he had never worn.

He sneezed, and his sneeze moved the flame of the torch he held so it wiggled and almost went out.

The soldier mannequin shook his head.

He pretended to look up at the ceiling.

The woman who didn't know she had kicked dust through cracks in the warped wooden floorboards backed up against the wall.

The soldier mannequin reached his hand toward the ceiling, searching for a trap door.

He felt a thick rope dangling from the ceiling and pulled it.

Other soldier mannequins bumped into him and stopped.

The trap door fell and the retractable ladder slid down, smashing the soldier mannequin's plastic face, caving it in.

The women saw torchlight burst through the opening trap door, cutting a bright, flickering square hole out of the floor's darkness.

They covered their children's eyes, closed their own.

One soldier mannequin stepped over the soldier mannequin whose face the attic ladder had caved in and climbed the attic ladder.

Others who had bumped into him followed.

They climbed slowly.

Their torches lit the attic.

Some soldier mannequins couldn't hold it in anymore, and they plunged their fingers down their throats, vomiting a piano sonata, the music splattering thick and white onto the attic's cold, warped wooden floorboards.

The women cringed.

They watched the mannequins in horror.

Their faces were blank, seemed eyeless.

Their bodies flickered like the shadows of wings flapping in the torchlight.

More climbed into the attic, groping the walls.

The women and children all huddled together, trembling.

Soldier mannequins approached them along both walls, from both sides of the attic.

One soldier mannequin groped the wall and the air in front of him.

A woman stood still as the soldier mannequin's hand got closer.

She closed her eyes and a tear squeezed out, a decapitated torch-lit reflection of the soldier mannequin's bald head.

Almost as the soldier mannequin's hand touched her cheek, the woman opened her eyes and moved her face a little.

The soldier mannequin missed.

His hand kept coming, and she moved her head again and, again, the soldier mannequin missed.

His hand again came for her and she couldn't move any farther away, and his hand brushed her cheek.

The soldier mannequin stopped.

His blank, lashless eyes got real big, and he tilted his bald head.

He opened his hand and felt the woman's face with his palm, with the tips of his fingers, and the woman began to cry, and her sobbing shook her, and the soldier mannequin moaned.

The soldier mannequin grabbed the woman's throat.

He stomped his foot, and the other soldier mannequins in the attic felt with their feet the vibrations of his foot stomping travel through the fibers of the floorboards' wood.

They followed the stomping.

The children cried.

The soldier mannequin clutched the woman's neck, squeezed.

Her son punched the soldier mannequin in the crotch, broke some of his fingers against the crotch's plastic flesh, and the child began to cry.

The soldier mannequin kicked the child in the tummy, and the child fell.

The soldier mannequin crushed the woman's throat—the windpipe within—between his fingers, and the woman fell to the floor beside her son.

Her son climbed on top of her and cried, trying to protect her, but she was already dead, and he cried.

The other women attacked the other soldier mannequins.

They jumped on their backs.

Some of the soldier mannequins dropped their torches, the flames like liquid leaking out onto the warped wooden floor of the attic.

The women hit them all over their naked bodies, and the soldier mannequins made fists and they put those fists through the women's bellies and their chests and their heads.

One soldier mannequin tore a woman's heart out—her heart still beating in his hand.

The flames like liquid leaking out of the fallen torches made little puddles, and the attic caught fire as their puddles spread, melding to become one big puddle.

Most of the other soldier mannequins were still downstairs.

They didn't know what was happening.

They groped their way back outside.

# REUNION

"You're here," Farmer said, "but you're not helping."

"Farmer, please," Quall said. "I feel really just awful."

"I don't care how you *feel*. Get into your sack and grab a goddamn hand grenade. You're making me mad."

Farmer vaulted himself through the mud on his crutches with his one leg left, a moving tripod squishing into the soggy ground.

He stopped sometimes to regain his balance.

He reached into his tattered burlap sack, pulled out hand grenades.

He took their pins in his teeth, bit them out.

Quall stood pouting as Farmer launched his hand grenades anywherever, and he blew up so many mannequins, and their limbs flew all over.

Quall could have run away.

He could have easily outrun Farmer with his one leg left—he could have run back to the colony, or he could have searched the mannequin compound for Jaundice.

All the other lepers who hadn't yet fallen apart in battle were blowing up everything they could.

Not Quall.

Quall followed Farmer.

He did nothing else.

He didn't want to risk one of his hand grenades landing near Jaundice and blowing her up.

If they saw Jaundice, Quall would maybe have a chance to stop Farmer.

Farmer stopped.

Quall stopped.

"What is it?" Quall said.

"Autocrates," Farmer said.

"Where?"

"His crutch."

Farmer vaulted toward the crutch, sticking up out of the mud.

Quall followed Farmer.

Farmer stopped at the crutch, touched it with his fingers.

He looked around.

Lepers and mannequins.

They all yelled things.

They moved around.

Through the smoke and fires illuminating the mannequin compound, Farmer saw Autocrates lying in the mud near a burning cabin.

His other leg was gone.

His prosthetic arm.

Farmer vaulted toward him.

Quall followed Farmer.

"Autocrates," Farmer called.

Autocrates sobbed, writhing around in the mud, moaning and feeling bad about himself.

"I had one good leg," he said.

"What happened?" Farmer said.

"My leg, it stepped on a goddamn hand grenade."

"Where's Mellon?"

"Last I saw him, his body was being blown to pieces over there…and there…and there."

Autocrates pointed to places with the fingers on the one hand on his one arm left.

Farmer puckered his lips and crunched his brows and, with his eyes, followed Autocrates' fingers to places Mellon or pieces of Mellon may or may not have been.

Quall looked around blankly, not to where Autocrates pointed but just anywherever, thinking: *Where is Jaundice…*

Farmer didn't want to kneel down to comfort Autocrates.

He thought it would be too difficult, too complicated a procedure, falling onto his one knee left and off his crutches, then afterward having to somehow get back up onto the crutches.

Farmer didn't want to get into all that.

There wasn't time.

Farmer touched Autocrates' face with the bottom of one of his crutches, carefully caressing his cheek.

He lost his balance, and jabbed the crutch into Autocrates' jaw.

"Sorry," Farmer said.

"Thank you, Farmer."

Autocrates died, his eyes and mouth widening as he inhaled a breath he never released.

Farmer put his head down, and a tear squeezed out one of his eyes.

He swung his head back and forth.

Quall didn't notice.

He looked around for Jaundice.

Farmer lifted his head, looked at Quall.

"Christ," he said. "Wake up, dickless wonder."

He whacked Quall with one of his crutches.

Quall snapped out of it, said, "What?"

"What do you mean, *What*? Autocrates is dead."

"You want me to write a play about it?"

Farmer looked at Quall.

"Let's move," Farmer said, vaulting away through the mud.

Quall followed him.

"There's nothing I could've done."

"Hand grenades, Quall."

Farmer stopped and reached into his sack, and he pulled out a hand grenade and he bit the pin out with his teeth and he threw the hand grenade somewherever.

"Farmer, I'm not going to do it."

"Because you don't want to destroy your love? She won't die, Quall. None of them die."

"Her dad's dead…" Quall said.

Farmer continued vaulting.

"…And I love her just the way she is…"

Farmer and Quall approached Clarice's cabin as Jaundice was coming out the back door.

"…And I don't want her to change."

Jaundice heard Quall's voice.

She ran around Clarice's cabin to find him, and she saw him, and he was there, with another leper, but she didn't know that until she had already called out: "Quall."

Farmer and Quall stopped.

Jaundice saw Farmer, and stopped.

"Jaundice," Quall said.

Farmer smiled, reaching into the mouth of his tattered burlap sack.

# DISPLAY

Clarice stood naked in the window, posing.

Jaundice's mom sat down.

"I don't know what's gotten into that girl," she said.

(There was Quall's penis to consider.)

"She wants to be like them," Clarice said.

Clarice looked at Jaundice's mom.

"I wish I could be her wishing I was someone else."

Jaundice's mom held her hands still on her lap.

Clarice looked back out the window.

She saw two lepers hobbling toward her cabin.

One of them vaulted through the mud on crutches.

The other had only one arm.

They appeared to be arguing.

Clarice watched them as they approached, and she heard a familiar voice call out: "Quall."

"Jaundice," Clarice said.

"What?" Jaundice's mom said.

"I think I heard Jaundice."

Clarice looked out the window.

The two lepers stopped.

One of them said, "Jaundice."

He had only one arm left.

The other had only one leg left and walked on crutches, and he was reaching into a tattered burlap sack slung over his shoulder.

Jaundice's mom got up and stood next to Clarice, looking out the window.

Farmer pulled out a hand grenade.

"Wait," Quall said.

He tried wrestling the hand grenade from Farmer's grip.

Jaundice backed away slowly.

She tripped over the root of a tree growing up out of the mud, and she fell backward.

Farmer whacked Quall in the ribs with his crutch where Quall's arm wasn't there anymore to block Farmer's crutch from whacking Quall in the ribs.

Quall bent over and fell to the ground, slipping and sloshing in the mud, holding his side with his one hand left.

"Quall," Jaundice called.

"Jaundice," Jaundice's mom called.

Farmer looked up at the cabin and saw two mannequins standing in the window.

He bit the pin out of the hand grenade and tossed it into the window and it went off, hurling Jaundice's mom's and Clarice's limbs out the window and just everywherever.

"Mom," Jaundice called, and she saw her mom's auburn wig floating like a torn parachute to the ground.

Farmer got another hand grenade from his tattered burlap sack and bit the pin out.

He held the lever, clutching it in his fist.

He vaulted toward Jaundice lying there in the mud.

"No," Quall called on his knees, his one hand left holding his side where Farmer's whack still hurt.

"Open your mouth," Farmer said.

Jaundice closed her eyes, bit her lips.

"I said open your mouth."

Quall rose to his feet, came up behind Farmer.

Farmer turned a little, vaulting sideways toward Jaundice.

"Stop right there, Quall."

Quall stopped.

"Leave her alone," he said.

"I will, as soon as she opens her mouth."

"Don't do it, Jaundice."

"So, *this* is Jaundice. Oh, she's pretty. This *thing* is what you broke yourself off inside?"

Jaundice began to cry a little.

"There, there little booby," Farmer said, stroking Jaundice's brunette wig with the hand grenade.

He looked at Quall, said, "You look like you could use a hand. A whole arm, maybe."

Farmer stood up straight, held his head high.

Quall looked at Jaundice.

Jaundice, that's me.

Jaundice looked at Quall.

I looked at Quall.

"Tell you what," Farmer said. "I won't blow up your little life-sized doll here, if you just take what you need from her."

"Take what? What do you mean?"

"Her arm, Quall. Take her arm."

"I… I won't…"

"You will, or I'll have her in pieces all over the place, and the rest of us'll take what we need. It might as well be you."

Quall and Jaundice looked at one another.

"It would be more…romantic that way," Farmer said.

"I… I can't…"

"Do it."

Quall hobbled toward Jaundice lying in the mud.

"Quall, no," Jaundice said.

Farmer smiled real big.

Quall got down on his knees.

He didn't look at Jaundice.

He grabbed her elbow with his hand, with his one hand left, and broke her arm out of its socket, ripping her arm off—the arm Jaundice would have offered Quall in the woods, if she had not been so upset and offered him the wrong arm.

"Good boy," Farmer said.

Jaundice cried a little.

She got up and ran away through smoke toward the stone tower.

"Let her go," Farmer said. "Try the arm on."

Quall watched Jaundice disappear into the smoke.

He closed his eyes, lowered his head.

He stuck Jaundice's arm into his shoulder socket, and all the rotted flesh there seemed to sprout tendrils—thin withered vines like caterpillars crawling onto the shoulder of Jaundice's arm, clinging to the new appendage.

The caterpillars, like fingers, began to cross, weaving into and around one another like wicker, their skin fusing, growing like that over Jaundice's arm's shoulder.

Quall began to cry a little.

"Looks good on you," Farmer said.

Quall looked at Farmer, stood up.

He kicked Farmer's knee, the one knee on Farmer's one leg left, and he kicked it so hard it went backwards, hyper-extended, like an ostrich leg.

"Ahhhhhh," Farmer said. "Christ."

He dropped his crutches and toppled over.

The hand grenade rolled out of his fist.

Quall grabbed the hand grenade with Jaundice's arm, the hand on Jaundice's arm, clutching the lever before it popped.

"You look hungry," he said.

"Goddamn you, Quall."

Quall kicked Farmer in the ribs.

"Ahhhhhhh," Farmer went.

Quall released the lever and shoved the hand grenade like a dark green jellybean hard into Farmer's mouth, and the hand grenade broke some of his teeth off, out, into and down his throat.

Quall shoved the dark green jellybean into Farmer's mouth so hard and deep Farmer's jaw opened too wide, dislocated, and made a loud cracking sound.

He couldn't spit the hand grenade out, his eyes bulging, watering as he choked on his teeth.

Quall hobbled away to find Jaundice.

He thought about having children.

# THE END

The attic was on fire.

Women.

Children.

Mannequins.

Their bodies all burned.

The fire consumed the attic walls, spread to the ceiling and ate through that, too, the roof opening like the mouth of a leper's tattered burlap sack.

The rain did nothing to put the fire out.

The wind was having its birthday.

It blew on the attic fire, but the attic fire was a trick candle stuck in the colony's cake and wouldn't go out.

The fire leapt to another shack.

Another shack.

Another.

The fire leapt all over the colony.

The cake waited for a wish.

The soldier mannequins never thought about birthdays.

They had never had any.

The soldier mannequins—who were all the same age as all the other mannequins, who were all the same age as the now ageless tribal elders—groped their way back toward the colony's entrance.

The soldier mannequins who had found the colony's water source, who had contaminated it, were just leaving, too.

Their plastic feet sloshed through the mud and, though they felt one another's footsteps jiggling shockwaves through the mud, they still bumped into each other as they fled the colony into the woods.

Rain pelted their naked bodies as they groped the trees.

All the lepers left had fled the mannequin compound, hobbling back through the woods toward the colony.

They had gathered all the mannequin limbs they could carry in their empty burlap sacks.

They were tired, cold, hungry, and they just wanted to go

home and rebuild themselves.

This thought was the only thing that kept them going.

Just before dawn, near the small stream where Mellon found Quall's arm, where Bayer's body still lay, one leper, half asleep, looked out into the darkness and saw shadows flickering through the trees.

"Mannequins," he called.

All the lepers left, all half asleep, stopped, blinking wide eyes to wake up, squinting to focus.

Some soldier mannequins still carried torches, which didn't matter because they couldn't see anyway, and it didn't matter they couldn't see because it was night, and daylight would have been enough light to see by without torches, but they couldn't see.

"Mannequins," another leper called.

All the lepers left hobbled quickly down the hill.

Their full burlap sacks were emptied of hand grenades.

Their empty burlap sacks were now full of harvested mannequin limbs.

They never found the rumored warehouse, the fabled surplus room, but they blew up all the mannequins they could and harvested their limbs.

The soldier mannequins felt the ground trembling.

They felt the mud jiggling under their bare feet, squishing between their plastic toes.

All the lepers left pulled harvested mannequin limbs from their tattered burlap sacks, and they raised them in the air as they hobbled down the hill toward the soldier mannequins.

"Rip their goddamn heads off," one leper said.

"Heartless bastards," another leper said.

"If they won't die, we'll kill them all," another leper said.

The soldier mannequins stood still as the lepers approached.

The lepers swung harvested mannequin limbs and the soldier mannequins ducked or caught the limbs as the lepers swung them.

Some lepers swung harvested mannequin limbs at the side of a soldier mannequin's bald head and knocked him over.

They ripped the soldier mannequin to pieces, yanking his arms and legs out, off, and hurling them everywherever.

One leper crushed a soldier mannequin's bald head under his foot wrapped in a cloth bootie, shattering the bone of his heel.

Other lepers smashed other soldier mannequins' bald heads with harvested mannequin limbs while other soldier mannequins punched holes through other lepers' chests and ripped their hearts out and tore them to pieces.

The sky soon went from black to gray.

The moon's cork was pulled out, and the sun was a big hole

at the top of the bottle their world was, and some light poured into the bottle, but inside the bottle was still mostly all clouds and mist.

Lepers and mannequins.

This was how they spent their morning.

Then they all stopped.

There were no more lepers.

There were no more mannequins.

Under the bare limbs of trees in the woods where new wet leaves were just beginning to unfurl the veiny palms of their hands, they lay in pieces: All the lepers and all the mannequins—they all fell apart together.

There were no more lepers and there were no more mannequins left standing to do anything else to each other there in the woods near the small stream where Jaundice and Quall once loved each other.

# FIREWORKS

Only two lepers remained at Lodge IV.

The compound was littered with human and mannequin bodies and parts of human and mannequin bodies, and it made Jaundice start to cry a little more, and it made Quall feel really just awful.

Jaundice had fled through smoke toward the stone tower, and Quall hobbled after her and away from Farmer's mouth vomiting the hand grenade's explosion.

Quall reached the stone tower's entrance and looked into its stairway, the walls wet with rain trickling in through moss-filled cracks in the stone.

He saw nothing but human and mannequin bodies and parts of human and mannequin bodies strewn just everywherever.

It was too much, too cluttered all the way up the stone stairway for Quall to climb.

He heard someone screaming in the tower.

He hobbled outside and looked up at the tower's only window, a paneless window.

"Quall," the voice called.

Quall looked around.

There were nothing but bodies and parts of bodies.

He raised his arm, his new arm—Jaundice's arm—, and he looked at it.

He looked at its hand.

He wiggled its fingers.

Quall began collecting all the human and mannequin arms he could find lying around the stone tower's stairway.

Quall picked up two arms: One human, one mannequin.

He wrapped the fingers of the mannequin arm's hand around the human arm's shoulder, the human arm's shoulder's skin fusing with the plastic flesh of the mannequin arm's hand's fingers.

Quall picked up another mannequin arm and made that one's hand grab and hold onto another human arm's shoulder, their fleshes fusing, forming a rope out of all the human and mannequin arms.

Jaundice screamed from the tower.

Quall looked up at the window.

He finished making the rope of human and mannequin arms and hobbled outside through the stone archway.

He stood under the window and swung the rope of arms in a circle over his head.

He flung the rope up and the first arm's hand, a mannequin hand, grabbed hold of the windowsill.

He pulled the arms taut and, carefully, he began to climb them.

Quall reached the window and grabbed the sill's ledge with his one hand left, then with Jaundice's hand.

He pulled himself up some so he could see over the ledge and into the window where he found Soren shoving Jaundice to the floor near a fireplace, their shadows flickering on the walls.

Quall climbed into the window as they struggled.

"Leave her alone," he said.

"Quall," Jaundice said.

"Quall?" Soren said.

Soren grabbed Jaundice's one arm left and pulled her in front of him.

"This must be the one you fancy," he said.

Jaundice began to cry a little more.

"Let her go," Quall said.

Soren clutched the only hand grenade he had left, pulled the pin out with his teeth.

He spit the pin toward Quall, and one of his teeth flew out with the pin.

"Christ," Soren said, covering his mouth, some blood dribbling down his chin.

He wrapped the arm he clutched the hand grenade in around Jaundice's neck, squeezing the hand grenade's lever.

He put his other arm's hand on one of Jaundice's breasts.

He massaged it, his palm sweaty.

He rubbed his crotch against Jaundice's rear end.

"I can see why you'd like this, Quall."

"I said let her go."

"It feels pretty good. I'm getting a little hard over here."

Soren fondled Jaundice's breast, licked her neck.

Jaundice felt Soren's penis growing, pressing into her rear end.

Soren got some of Jaundice's brunette wig hair in his mouth.

He snatched the wig off her head.

He licked the side of her face.

"Goddamn it, Soren," Quall said.

"I could totally dig this mannequin of yours, Quall. Only thing is, I hate her tits. No nipples. They don't even move."

Jaundice burst into tears.

"Hey, little lady," Soren said.

Jaundice elbowed Soren in the belly, and she punched him in his crotch with her one arm left, her one hand, her one plastic fist, crunching Soren's hardening penis into itself like an accordion backward into his balls.

Soren doubled over, fell to the floor, still clutching the hand grenade.

Jaundice ran toward the fireplace.

Quall hobbled over to Soren and, with his one arm left that was his and Jaundice's arm, picked Soren up off the floor and, by the shirt and the rope wound and tied around Soren's waist, pulled Soren toward the window and threw Soren, still clutching the hand grenade, through the window.

Jaundice ran to Quall and hugged him and, just as they hugged, they kissed and, just as they kissed, there was an explosion outside.

# ADOPTION

Jaundice picked up her brunette wig and put it back on her head.

She climbed onto Quall's back and wrapped her one arm left around his chest as Quall climbed down the rope of human and mannequin arms hanging from the stone tower's windowsill.

They looked around.

There was nothing.

Nothing but smoke, and there were bodies and parts of bodies lying all over the place and just everywherever.

Quall put his arm, his new arm—Jaundice's arm—, around Jaundice.

He kissed her cheek.

Jaundice took Quall's hand, his one hand he had left that was really his, and they walked around looking for anything still alive, still moving.

There was nothing.

"I'm sorry," Quall said.

Jaundice smiled big.

"It's okay."

"It's not okay," Quall said.

"It's what we mannequins wanted."

"I don't understand."

"I want to show you something."

Jaundice pulled Quall by his one hand left that was really his into the main hall—what was left of it.

They found bodies and parts of bodies floating in the small stream flowing through the middle of the hall, so many body parts they formed a dam clogging the stream so the water stopped falling down the well in front of where the elders' table once was and began flooding the hall—the elders' white wigs, too, all floating in the water.

"Is that *our* stream?" Quall said.

"Shhh," Jaundice said, and she put her finger over Quall's lips.

She led Quall toward the far end of the main hall, to a stone wall.

"What's this?" he said.

Jaundice pushed the stone wall hard as she could, and the stone wall moved, the stone of the bottom of the wall scraping against the stone of the floor, and she pushed it harder and it moved more, and she pushed the stone wall all the way open.

"Come on," she said.

They entered a dark room, and Jaundice felt around in the air with her one hand left and found in front of her a thick rope dangling from the ceiling.

She pulled the rope and bright lights burst on, illuminating the big room: A warehouse with big wooden shelves stretching floor to ceiling stacked against crumbling stone walls, rain trickling in through moss-filled cracks.

On the shelves were nothing but spare parts.

Mannequin parts.

Quall opened his mouth.

Jaundice smiled bigger.

"I thought it was just a rumor," Quall said.

The room was so big, and it seemed to circle Quall, spinning around him like a Ferris wheel that had fallen over drunk, and he tried following it, to compensate for its spinning, but he still got dizzy.

"Nope," Jaundice said. "It's real."

Jaundice.

That's me.

I'm Jaundice.

I knew now.

"My mom," I said. "She tried to tell me… We were once like you."

Quall looked around at all the arms and all the legs and all the torsos and all the heads lining the shelves, all different sizes.

"You mean…*human*?" he said.

"This is how we all stay the same age, I think."

"So, your whole tribe, you can just—"

"Yes," I said.

"Did you build our colony, long ago?"

"Not me, personally."

On the ends of some shelves, of the long rows of mannequin arms and legs and torsos and heads, Quall noticed loaves of brown bread, and on the ends of others he saw tattered burlap sacks.

He walked over to a shelf, untied the rope wound around one sack's mouth.

It was full of hand grenades, and he picked one up with my arm, looking at the hand grenade, looking at my hand holding it.

He stuffed the hand grenade back into the tattered burlap

sack's mouth.

He looked around and saw what appeared to be rows of shotgun shells on one of the shelves.

"What are those?" he said.

"Oh, lipstick," I said excitedly.

I walked over to the shelf with tubes of lipstick on it, picked one up.

I looked at it carefully, then put it back on the shelf.

"I don't think I need this anymore," I said.

Quall grabbed his arm, his new arm—my arm.

"Here," he said, tugging the arm, but all the tendrils of flesh that had overgrown the arm's shoulder like vines crawling like caterpillars—their fingers would not let go.

"Don't be silly," I said.

"Please. I feel really just awful about it."

"You keep it."

"But…"

"I already have something of yours."

Quall's eyes got real big.

"I'm pregnant with it…"

Quall looked at my crotch and smiled—I think I blushed a bit.

"…And I always will be. So I want you to keep something of mine."

I kissed Quall on the lips, and I opened my mouth, and I stuck my tongue into Quall's mouth and Quall stuck his tongue into my mouth, and our tongues licked each other all over.

I stopped kissing Quall, leaned back a bit, licked his lips with my tongue, teasing.

I smiled and went to one of the shelves with mannequin arms on it, and I reached up and pulled down an arm that looked just like mine.

# THE WOODS

Quall and I decided to leave Lodge IV's compound.

Quall thought we should quest for the leper colony to see what had happened there, what was left of anything.

We spent the day hiking and hobbling through the woods.

The rain got heavy, then light.

Halfway to the colony we came to our stream.

We looked around at all the human and mannequin bodies and parts of human and mannequin bodies, and everything was still—nothing was still alive, still moving.

Smoke drifting from Lodge IV, or from the colony, or from somewherever, filled the forest air.

Quall and I looked at each other.

We didn't say anything.

The sun was setting, the sky going black in some spots.

In those last moments of light, I saw something sparkling near my feet.

I crouched and picked the sparkling thing up, brushing wet leaves off it.

"My diamond bracelet," I said. "I thought I'd never find it."

Quall smiled and took my hand, and he clasped the diamond bracelet around my wrist.

Quall kissed me, and I kissed Quall.

We followed our stream until we found a place in the woods that wasn't littered with human and mannequin bodies and parts of human and mannequin bodies, and we made a nice place to sleep out of wet leaves, and we slept.

In the morning, we began again toward the colony.

We didn't expect to find anything much different when we got there.

As we approached the colony, Quall thought he saw something.

"I can't believe it," he said.

I squinted, trying to see.

"What is that?" I said.

"Christ—"

Quall hobbled to the colony's entrance just as Farmer's mannequin was crawling on all fours away from it.

They reached one another, and Farmer's mannequin leapt up into Quall's arms—his one arm left and my arm—and hugged Quall.

Quall pet Farmer's mannequin's bald head.

"Hey boy, how are you?" he said, though Quall just now realized he'd never actually known Farmer's mannequin's gender (sans genitals, as it was—though, too, sans breast-shaped mounds adorning its chest…).

Farmer's mannequin was burned all over with dark brown spots where the fire charred its plastic body and melted small black holes into some of it.

"What did they do to you?"

"Who's this?" I said.

"Farmer's mannequin."

I touched Farmer's mannequin's head.

Quall put Farmer's mannequin down.

Farmer's mannequin took my hand in its hand.

The three of us, me and Quall and Farmer's mannequin, we entered the colony.

Quall and I looked around.

Farmer's mannequin rubbed its bald head up against Quall's leg.

The whole colony had burned down.

There was nothing left.

Smoke rose off the piles of ash that used to be shacks before they burned down, but were now just piles of ash that used to be shacks that burned down.

Rain fell lightly.

I noticed a flower growing up out of the mud.

A bee landed on the flower, its wings glistening.

Quall and I looked at each other.

"Where should we live, now?" I said.

Jaundice.

That's me.

I'm Jaundice.

I said that.

I wanted to know where we should live.

"I don't know," Quall said.

"The woods?" I said.

"I know a perfect place, a soft patch of wet leaves near a small stream."

"Sounds pretty."

"It's nice."

## ABOUT THE AUTHOR

Eric Beeny (b. 1981) is the author of *The Dying Bloom* (Pangur Ban Party, 2009), *Snowing Fireflies* (Folded Word Press, 2010), *Of Creatures* (Gold Wake Press, 2010), *Milk Like a Melted Ghost* (Thumbscrews Press, 2011), *Pseudo-Masochism* (Anonymosity Press, 2011) and *How Much the Jaw Weighs* (Anonymosity Press, 2011). His blog is *Dead End on Progressive Ave*. (http://ericbeeny.blogspot.com).

# BIZARRO BOOKS

## CATALOG FALL 2011

ERASERHEAD PRESS

Swallowdown Press

FUNGASM

LAZY FASCIST

Your major resource for the bizarro fiction genre:

**WWW.BIZARROCENTRAL.COM**

Introduce yourselves to the bizarro fiction genre and all of its authors with the Bizarro Starter Kit series. Each volume features short novels and short stories by ten of the leading bizarro authors, designed to give you a perfect sampling of the genre for only $10.

**BB-0X1**
**"The Bizarro Starter Kit" (Orange)**
Featuring D. Harlan Wilson, Carlton Mellick III, Jeremy Robert Johnson, Kevin L Donihe, Gina Ranalli, Andre Duza, Vincent W. Sakowski, Steve Beard, John Edward Lawson, and Bruce Taylor.
**236 pages $10**

**BB-0X2**
**"The Bizarro Starter Kit" (Blue)**
Featuring Ray Fracalossy, Jeremy C. Shipp, Jordan Krall, Mykle Hansen, Andersen Prunty, Eckhard Gerdes, Bradley Sands, Steve Aylett, Christian TeBordo, and Tony Rauch. **244 pages $10**

**BB-0X2**
**"The Bizarro Starter Kit" (Purple)**
Featuring Russell Edson, Athena Villaverde, David Agranoff, Matthew Revert, Andrew Goldfarb, Jeff Burk, Garrett Cook, Kris Saknussemm, Cody Goodfellow, and Cameron Pierce **264 pages $10**

BB-001**"The Kafka Effekt" D. Harlan Wilson** — A collection of forty-four irreal short stories loosely written in the vein of Franz Kafka, with more than a pinch of William S. Burroughs sprinkled on top. **211 pages $14**

BB-002 **"Satan Burger" Carlton Mellick III** — The cult novel that put Carlton Mellick III on the map ... Six punks get jobs at a fast food restaurant owned by the devil in a city violently overpopulated by surreal alien cultures. **236 pages $14**

BB-003 **"Some Things Are Better Left Unplugged" Vincent Sakwoski** — Join The Man and his Nemesis, the obese tabby, for a nightmare roller coaster ride into this postmodern fantasy. **152 pages $10**

BB-004 **"Shall We Gather At the Garden?" Kevin L Donihe** — Donihe's Debut novel. Midgets take over the world, The Church of Lionel Richie vs. The Church of the Byrds, plant porn and more! **244 pages $14**

BB-005 **"Razor Wire Pubic Hair" Carlton Mellick III** — A genderless humandildo is purchased by a razor dominatrix and brought into her nightmarish world of bizarre sex and mutilation. **176 pages $11**

BB-006 **"Stranger on the Loose" D. Harlan Wilson** — The fiction of Wilson's 2nd collection is planted in the soil of normalcy, but what grows out of that soil is a dark, witty, otherworldly jungle... **228 pages $14**

BB-007 **"The Baby Jesus Butt Plug" Carlton Mellick III** — Using clones of the Baby Jesus for anal sex will be the hip sex fetish of the future. **92 pages $10**

BB-008 **"Fishyfleshed" Carlton Mellick III** — The world of the past is an illogical flatland lacking in dimension and color, a sick-scape of crispy squid people wandering the desert for no apparent reason. **260 pages $14**

BB-009 **"Dead Bitch Army" Andre Duza** — Step into a world filled with racist teenagers, cannibals, 100 warped Uncle Sams, automobiles with razor-sharp teeth, living graffiti, and a pissed-off zombie bitch out for revenge. **344 pages $16**

BB-010 **"The Menstruating Mall" Carlton Mellick III** — "The Breakfast Club meets Chopping Mall as directed by David Lynch." - Brian Keene **212 pages $12**

BB-011 **"Angel Dust Apocalypse" Jeremy Robert Johnson** — Meth-heads, man-made monsters, and murderous Neo-Nazis. "Seriously amazing short stories..." - Chuck Palahniuk, author of Fight Club **184 pages $11**

BB-012 **"Ocean of Lard" Kevin L Donihe / Carlton Mellick III** — A parody of those old Choose Your Own Adventure kid's books about some very odd pirates sailing on a sea made of animal fat. **176 pages $12**

BB-015 **"Foop!" Chris Genoa** — Strange happenings are going on at Dactyl, Inc, the world's first and only time travel tourism company.
"A surreal pie in the face!" - Christopher Moore **300 pages $14**

**BB-020 "Punk Land" Carlton Mellick III** — In the punk version of Heaven, the anarchist utopia is threatened by corporate fascism and only Goblin, Mortician's sperm, and a blue-mohawked female assassin named Shark Girl can stop them. **284 pages $15**

BB-027 **"Siren Promised" Jeremy Robert Johnson & Alan M Clark** — Nominated for the Bram Stoker Award. A potent mix of bad drugs, bad dreams, brutal bad guys, and surreal/incredible art by Alan M. Clark. **190 pages $13**

BB-031 **"Sea of the Patchwork Cats" Carlton Mellick III** — A quiet dreamlike tale set in the ashes of the human race. For Mellick enthusiasts who also adore The Twilight Zone. **112 pages $10**

BB-032 **"Extinction Journals" Jeremy Robert Johnson** — An uncanny voyage across a newly nuclear America where one man must confront the problems associated with loneliness, insane dieties, radiation, love, and an ever-evolving cockroach suit with a mind of its own. **104 pages $10**

BB-037 **"The Haunted Vagina" Carlton Mellick III** — It's difficult to love a woman whose vagina is a gateway to the world of the dead. **132 pages $10**

BB-043 **"War Slut" Carlton Mellick III** — Part "1984," part "Waiting for Godot," and part action horror video game adaptation of John Carpenter's "The Thing." **116 pages $10**

BB-047 **"Sausagey Santa" Carlton Mellick III** — A bizarro Christmas tale featuring Santa as a piratey mutant with a body made of sausages. 124 pages $10

BB-048 **"Misadventures in a Thumbnail Universe" Vincent Sakowski** — Dive deep into the surreal and satirical realms of neo-classical Blender Fiction, filled with television shoes and flesh-filled skies. **120 pages $10**

BB-053 **"Ballad of a Slow Poisoner" Andrew Goldfarb** — Millford Mutterwurst sat down on a Tuesday to take his afternoon tea, and made the unpleasant discovery that his elbows were becoming flatter. **128 pages $10**

BB-055 **"Help! A Bear is Eating Me" Mykle Hansen** — The bizarro, heart-warming, magical tale of poor planning, hubris and severe blood loss...
**150 pages $11**

BB-056 **"Piecemeal June" Jordan Krall** — A man falls in love with a living sex doll, but with love comes danger when her creator comes after her with crab-squid assassins. **90 pages $9**

BB-058 **"The Overwhelming Urge" Andersen Prunty** — A collection of bizarro tales by Andersen Prunty. **150 pages $11**

BB-059 **"Adolf in Wonderland" Carlton Mellick III** — A dreamlike adventure that takes a young descendant of Adolf Hitler's design and sends him down the rabbit hole into a world of imperfection and disorder. **180 pages $11**

BB-061 **"Ultra Fuckers" Carlton Mellick III** — Absurdist suburban horror about a couple who enter an upper middle class gated community but can't find their way out. **108 pages $9**

BB-062 **"House of Houses" Kevin L. Donihe** — An odd man wants to marry his house. Unfortunately, all of the houses in the world collapse at the same time in the Great House Holocaust. Now he must travel to House Heaven to find his departed fiancee. **172 pages $11**

BB-064 **"Squid Pulp Blues" Jordan Krall** — In these three bizarro-noir novellas, the reader is thrown into a world of murderers, drugs made from squid parts, deformed gun-toting veterans, and a mischievous apocalyptic donkey. **204 pages $12**

BB-065 **"Jack and Mr. Grin" Andersen Prunty** — "When Mr. Grin calls you can hear a smile in his voice. Not a warm and friendly smile, but the kind that seizes your spine in fear. You don't need to pay your phone bill to hear it. That smile is in every line of Prunty's prose." - Tom Bradley. **208 pages $12**

BB-066 **"Cybernetrix" Carlton Mellick III** — What would you do if your normal everyday world was slowly mutating into the video game world from Tron? **212 pages $12**

BB-072 **"Zerostrata" Andersen Prunty** — Hansel Nothing lives in a tree house, suffers from memory loss, has a very eccentric family, and falls in love with a woman who runs naked through the woods every night. **144 pages $11**

BB-073 **"The Egg Man" Carlton Mellick III** — It is a world where humans reproduce like insects. Children are the property of corporations, and having an enormous ten-foot brain implanted into your skull is a grotesque sexual fetish. Mellick's industrial urban dystopia is one of his darkest and grittiest to date. **184 pages $11**

BB-074 **"Shark Hunting in Paradise Garden" Cameron Pierce** — A group of strange humanoid religious fanatics travel back in time to the Garden of Eden to discover it is invested with hundreds of giant flying maneating sharks. **150 pages $10**

BB-075 **"Apeshit" Carlton Mellick III** - Friday the 13th meets Visitor Q. Six hipster teens go to a cabin in the woods inhabited by a deformed killer. An incredibly fucked-up parody of B-horror movies with a bizarro slant. **192 pages $12**

BB-076 **"Fuckers of Everything on the Crazy Shitting Planet of the Vomit At smosphere" Mykle Hansen** - Three bizarro satires. Monster Cocks, Journey to the Center of Agnes Cuddlebottom, and Crazy Shitting Planet. **228 pages $12**

BB-077 **"The Kissing Bug" Daniel Scott Buck** — In the tradition of Roald Dahl, Tim Burton, and Edward Gorey, comes this bizarro anti-war children's story about a bohemian conenose kissing bug who falls in love with a human woman. **116 pages $10**

BB-078 **"MachoPoni" Lotus Rose** — It's My Little Pony... *Bizarro* style! A long time ago Poniworld was split in two. On one side of the Jagged Line is the Pastel Kingdom, a magical land of music, parties, and positivity. On the other side of the Jagged Line is Dark Kingdom inhabited by an army of undead ponies. **148 pages $11**

BB-079 **"The Faggiest Vampire" Carlton Mellick III** — A Roald Dahl-esque children's story about two faggy vampires who partake in a mustache competition to find out which one is truly the faggiest. **104 pages $10**

BB-080 **"Sky Tongues" Gina Ranalli** — The autobiography of Sky Tongues, the biracial hermaphrodite actress with tongues for fingers. Follow her strange life story as she rises from freak to fame. **204 pages $12**

BB-081 **"Washer Mouth" Kevin L. Donihe** - A washing machine becomes human and pursues his dream of meeting his favorite soap opera star. **244 pages $11**

BB-082 **"Shatnerquake" Jeff Burk** - All of the characters ever played by William Shatner are suddenly sucked into our world. Their mission: hunt down and destroy the real William Shatner. **100 pages $10**

BB-083 **"The Cannibals of Candyland" Carlton Mellick III** - There exists a race of cannibals that are made of candy. They live in an underground world made out of candy. One man has dedicated his life to killing them all. **170 pages $11**

BB-084 **"Slub Glub in the Weird World of the Weeping Willows" Andrew Goldfarb** - The charming tale of a blue glob named Slub Glub who helps the weeping willows whose tears are flooding the earth. There are also hyenas, ghosts, and a voodoo priest **100 pages $10**

BB-085 **"Super Fetus" Adam Pepper** - Try to abort this fetus and he'll kick your ass! **104 pages $10**

BB-086 **"Fistful of Feet" Jordan Krall** - A bizarro tribute to spaghetti westerns, featuring Cthulhu-worshipping Indians, a woman with four feet, a crazed gunman who is obsessed with sucking on candy, Syphilis-ridden mutants, sexually transmitted tattoos, and a house devoted to the freakiest fetishes. **228 pages $12**

BB-087 **"Ass Goblins of Auschwitz" Cameron Pierce** - It's Monty Python meets Nazi exploitation in a surreal nightmare as can only be imagined by Bizarro author Cameron Pierce. **104 pages $10**

BB-088 **"Silent Weapons for Quiet Wars" Cody Goodfellow** - "This is high-end psychological surrealist horror meets bottom-feeding low-life crime in a techno-thrilling science fiction world full of Lovecraft and magic..." -John Skipp **212 pages $12**

BB-089 **"Warrior Wolf Women of the Wasteland" Carlton Mellick III** — Road Warrior Werewolves versus McDonaldland Mutants...post-apocalyptic fiction has never been quite like this. **316 pages $13**

BB-091 **"Super Giant Monster Time" Jeff Burk** — A tribute to choose your own adventures and Godzilla movies. Will you escape the giant monsters that are rampaging the fuck out of your city and shit? Or will you join the mob of alien-controlled punk rockers causing chaos in the streets? What happens next depends on you. **188 pages $12**

BB-092 **"Perfect Union" Cody Goodfellow** — "Cronenberg's THE FLY on a grand scale: human/insect gene-spliced body horror, where the human hive politics are as shocking as the gore." -John Skipp. **272 pages $13**

BB-093 **"Sunset with a Beard" Carlton Mellick III** — 14 stories of surreal science fiction. **200 pages $12**

BB-094 **"My Fake War" Andersen Prunty** — The absurd tale of an unlikely soldier forced to fight a war that, quite possibly, does not exist. It's Rambo meets Waiting for Godot in this subversive satire of American values and the scope of the human imagination. **128 pages $11**

BB-095 **"Lost in Cat Brain Land" Cameron Pierce** — Sad stories from a surreal world. A fascist mustache, the ghost of Franz Kafka, a desert inside a dead cat. Primordial entities mourn the death of their child. The desperate serve tea to mysterious creatures. A hopeless romantic falls in love with a pterodactyl. And much more. **152 pages $11**

BB-096 **"The Kobold Wizard's Dildo of Enlightenment +2" Carlton Mellick III** — A Dungeons and Dragons parody about a group of people who learn they are only made up characters in an AD&D campaign and must find a way to resist their nerdy teenaged players and retarded dungeon master in order to survive. 232 **pages $12**

BB-098 **"A Hundred Horrible Sorrows of Ogner Stump" Andrew Goldfarb** — Goldfarb's acclaimed comic series. A magical and weird journey into the horrors of everyday life. **164 pages $11**

**BB-099 "Pickled Apocalypse of Pancake Island" Cameron Pierce**—A demented fairy tale about a pickle, a pancake, and the apocalypse. **102 pages $8**

**BB-100 "Slag Attack" Andersen Prunty**— Slag Attack features four visceral, noir stories about the living, crawling apocalypse.A slag is what survivors are calling the slug-like maggots raining from the sky, burrowing inside people, and hollowing out their flesh and their sanity. **148 pages $11**

**BB-101 "Slaughterhouse High" Robert Devereaux**—A place where schools are built with secret passageways, rebellious teens get zippers installed in their mouths and genitals, and once a year, on that special night, one couple is slaughtered and the bits of their bodies are kept as souvenirs. **304 pages $13**

**BB-102 "The Emerald Burrito of Oz" John Skipp & Marc Levinthal** —OZ IS REAL! Magic is real! The gate is really in Kansas! And America is finally allowing Earth tourists to visit this weird-ass, mysterious land. But when Gene of Los Angeles heads off for summer vacation in the Emerald City, little does he know that a war is brewing...a war that could destroy both worlds. **280 pages $13**

**BB-103 "The Vegan Revolution... with Zombies" David Agranoff** — When there's no more meat in hell, the vegans will walk the earth. **160 pages $11**

**BB-104 "The Flappy Parts" Kevin L Donihe**—Poems about bunnies, LSD, and police abuse. You know, things that matter. 132 **pages $11**

**BB-105 "Sorry I Ruined Your Orgy" Bradley Sands**—Bizarro humorist Bradley Sands returns with one of the strangest, most hilarious collections of the year. **130 pages $11**

**BB-106 "Mr. Magic Realism" Bruce Taylor**—Like Golden Age science fiction comics written by Freud, *Mr. Magic Realism* is a strange, insightful adventure that spans the furthest reaches of the galaxy, exploring the hidden caverns in the hearts and minds of men, women, aliens, and biomechanical cats. **152 pages $11**

BB-107 **"Zombies and Shit" Carlton Mellick III**—"Battle Royale" meets "Return of the Living Dead." Mellick's bizarro tribute to the zombie genre. **308 pages $13**

BB-108 **"The Cannibal's Guide to Ethical Living" Mykle Hansen**—Over a five star French meal of fine wine, organic vegetables and human flesh, a lunatic delivers a witty, chilling, disturbingly sane argument in favor of eating the rich.. **184 pages $11**

BB-109 **"Starfish Girl" Athena Villaverde**—In a post-apocalyptic underwater dome society, a girl with a starfish growing from her head and an assassin with sea anenome hair are on the run from a gang of mutant fish men. **160 pages $11**

BB-110 **"Lick Your Neighbor" Chris Genoa**—Mutant ninjas, a talking whale, kung fu masters, maniacal pilgrims, and an alcoholic clown populate Chris Genoa's surreal, darkly comical and unnerving reimagining of the first Thanksgiving. **303 pages $13**

BB-111 **"Night of the Assholes" Kevin L. Donihe**—A plague of assholes is infecting the countryside. Normal everyday people are transforming into jerks, snobs, dicks, and douchebags. And they all have only one purpose: to make your life a living hell.. **192 pages $11**

BB-112 **"Jimmy Plush, Teddy Bear Detective" Garrett Cook**—Hard-boiled cases of a private detective trapped within a teddy bear body. **180 pages $11**

BB-113 **"The Deadheart Shelters" Forrest Armstrong**—The hip hop lovechild of William Burroughs and Dali... **144 pages $11**

BB-114 **"Eyeballs Growing All Over Me... Again" Tony Raugh**—Absurd, surreal, playful, dream-like, whimsical, and a lot of fun to read. **144 pages $11**

**BB-115** **"Whargoul" Dave Brockie** — From the killing grounds of Stalingrad to the death camps of the holocaust. From torture chambers in Iraq to race riots in the United States, the Whargoul was there, killing and raping. **244 pages $12**

**BB-116** **"By the Time We Leave Here, We'll Be Friends" J. David Osborne** — A David Lynchian nightmare set in a Russian gulag, where its prisoners, guards, traitors, soldiers, lovers, and demons fight for survival and their own rapidly deteriorating humanity. **168 pages $11**

**BB-117** **"Christmas on Crack" edited by Carlton Mellick III** — Perverted Christmas Tales for the whole family! . . . as long as every member of your family is over the age of 18. **168 pages $11**

**BB-118** **"Crab Town" Carlton Mellick III** — Radiation fetishists, balloon people, mutant crabs, sail-bike road warriors, and a love affair between a woman and an H-Bomb. This is one mean asshole of a city. Welcome to Crab Town. **100 pages $8**

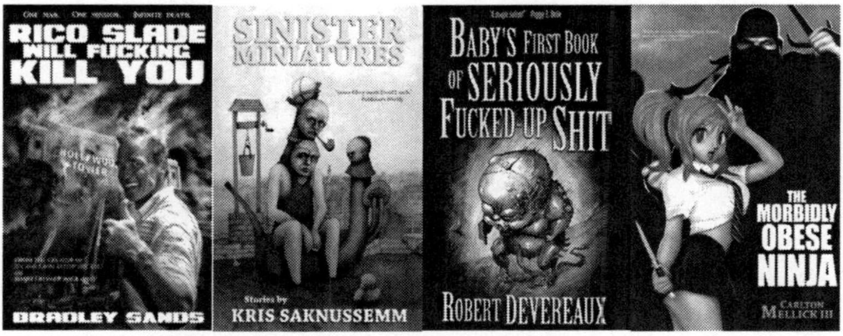


**BB-119** **"Rico Slade Will Fucking Kill You" Bradley Sands** — Rico Slade is an action hero. Rico Slade can rip out a throat with his bare hands. Rico Slade's favorite food is the honey-roasted peanut. Rico Slade will fucking kill everyone. A novel. **122 pages $8**

**BB-120** **"Sinister Miniatures" Kris Saknussemm** — The definitive collection of short fiction by Kris Saknussemm, confirming that he is one of the best, most daring writers of the weird to emerge in the twenty-first century. **180 pages $11**

**BB-121** **"Baby's First Book of Seriously Fucked up Shit" Robert Devereaux** — Ten stories of the strange, the gross, and the just plain fucked up from one of the most original voices in horror. **176 pages $11**

**BB-122** **"The Morbidly Obese Ninja" Carlton Mellick III** — These days, if you want to run a successful company . . . you're going to need a lot of ninjas. **92 pages $8**

BB-123 **"Abortion Arcade" Cameron Pierce** — An intoxicating blend of body horror and midnight movie madness, reminiscent of early David Lynch and the splatterpunks at their most sublime. **172 pages $11**

BB-124 **"Black Hole Blues" Patrick Wensink** — A hilarious double helix of country music and physics. **196 pages $11**

BB-125 **"Barbarian Beast Bitches of the Badlands" Carlton Mellick III** — Three prequels and sequels to *Warrior Wolf Women of the Wasteland*. **284 pages $13**

BB-126 **"The Traveling Dildo Salesman" Kevin L. Donihe** — A nightmare comedy about destiny, faith, and sex toys. Also featuring Donihe's most lurid and infamous short stories: *Milky Agitation, Two-Way Santa, The Helen Mower, Living Room Zombies,* and *Revenge of the Living Masturbation Rag*. **108 pages $8**

BB-127 **"Metamorphosis Blues" Bruce Taylor** — Enter a land of love beasts, intergalactic cowboys, and rock 'n roll. A land where Sears Catalogs are doorways to insanity and men keep mysterious black boxes. Welcome to the monstrous mind of Mr. Magic Realism. **136 pages $11**

BB-128 **"The Driver's Guide to Hitting Pedestrians" Andersen Prunty** — A pocket guide to the twenty-three most painful things in life, written by the most well-adjusted man in the universe. **108 pages $8**

BB-129 **"Island of the Super People" Kevin Shamel** — Four students and their anthropology professor journey to a remote island to study its indigenous population. But this is no ordinary native culture. They're super heroes and villains with flesh costumes and out-landish abilities like self-detonation, musical eyelashes, and microwave hands. **194 pages $11**

BB-130 **"Fantastic Orgy" Carlton Mellick III** — Shark Sex, mutant cats, and strange sexually transmitted diseases. Featuring the stories: *Candy-coated, Ear Cat, Fantastic Orgy, City Hobgoblins*, and *Porno in August*. **136 pages $9**

BB-131 **"Cripple Wolf" Jeff Burk** — Part man. Part wolf. 100% crippled. Also including *Punk Rock Nursing Home, Adrift with Space Badgers, Cook for Your Life, Just Another Day in the Park, Frosty and the Full Monty*, and *House of Cats*. **152 pages $10**

BB-132 **"I Knocked Up Satan's Daughter" Carlton Mellick III** — An adorable, violent, fantastical love story. A romantic comedy for the bizarro fiction reader. **152 pages $10**

BB-133 **"A Town Called Suckhole" David W. Barbee** — Far into the future, in the nuclear bowels of post-apocalyptic Dixie, there is a town. A town of derelict mobile homes, ancient junk, and mutant wildlife. A town of slack jawed rednecks who bask in the splendors of moonshine and mud boggin'. A town dedicated to the bloody and demented legacy of the Old South. A town called Suckhole. **144 pages $10**

BB-134 **"Cthulhu Comes to the Vampire Kingdom" Cameron Pierce** — What you'd get if H. P. Lovecraft wrote a Tim Burton animated film. **148 pages $11**

BB-135 **"I am Genghis Cum" Violet LeVoit** — From the savage Arctic tundra to post-partum mutations to your missing daughter's unmarked grave, join visionary madwoman Violet LeVoit in this non-stop eight-story onslaught of full-tilt Bizarro punk lit thrills. **124 pages $9**

BB-136 **"Haunt" Laura Lee Bahr** — A tripping-balls Los Angeles noir, where a mysterious dame drags you through a time-warping Bizarro hall of mirrors. **316 pages $13**

BB-137 **"Amazing Stories of the Flying Spaghetti Monster" edited by Cameron Pierce** — Like an all-spaghetti evening of Adult Swim, the Flying Spaghetti Monster will show you the many realms of His Noodly Appendage. Learn of those who worship him and the lives he touches in distant, mysterious ways. **228 pages $12**

BB-138 **"Wave of Mutilation" Douglas Lain** — A dream-pop exploration of modern architecture and the American identity, *Wave of Mutilation* is a Zen finger trap for the 21st century. **100 pages $8**

CPSIA information can be obtained at www.ICGtesting.com
Printed in the USA
BVOW041641030112

279704BV00001B/6/P

9 781621 050070